THE
SECOND
SORROWFUL
MYSTERY

A Mystery

BY
JONATHAN HARRINGTON

A Write Way Publishing Book

Copyright © 1999, Jonathan Harrington

Write Way Publishing
PO Box 441278
Aurora, CO 80044

First Edition; 1999

The author gratefully acknowledges permission to quote from Rosary Novenas to Our Lady by Charles V. Lacey©1983; Glencoe/ McGraw Hill

Step Eight and Nine of the Twelve Steps of Alcoholics Anonymous have been reprinted with permission of Alcoholics Anonymous World Services, Inc.

Queries regarding rights and permissions should be addressed to Write Way Publishing, PO Box 441278, Aurora, CO, 80044

ISBN 1-885173-37-7

1 2 3 4 5 6 7 8 9

Special thanks to: Elizabeth Curtis, whose careful reading of several stages of the manuscript is greatly appreciated; my editor and publisher, Dorrie O'Brien, who first lifted Danny O'Flaherty from the submissions pile and breathed life into him; Jean Fiedler, Lee Alprin, Janine Jones, Tom Piccirilli, and Anne Lawrence for their helpful suggestions; my wife, Wren, for her encouragement and support; and finally I dedicate this book to my son, Trevor Owen Harrington.

Prologue

"To prepare ourselves to celebrate the sacred mysteries, let us call to mind our sins."

Father O'Malley's gaze swept over the eight parishioners who stood in St. Bridget's Catholic Church. Lowering his head, he held the bridge of his nose between his thumb and forefinger and rubbed at the tension between his eyes.

He looked back up, struck his breast lightly with his balled fist, and led the congregation in reciting the penitential rite: "I confess to almighty God, and to you, my brothers and sisters, that I have sinned through my own fault."

Father O'Malley swept back his raven-black hair with a rough, reddish hand, more suited to a laborer than a priest. His squarish head sat on broad, muscular shoulders, and he had the solid build of a well-stacked bale of hay. His bushy eyebrows grew together dividing his high, sloped forehead from his dark, deep-set eyes, and the ruddy skin of his face and neck contrasted sharply with the glowing white band of his Roman collar.

Lowering his head again, the priest meditated for a moment on the difficult task ahead of him. Wednesday he would go to the bishop and release the burden he carried. Next Sunday he would make a public confession to his congregation.

Halfway down the aisle a table stood with the water, wine, and hosts. After the sermon, two parishioners brought the offertory gifts to the altar. Father O'Malley received the paten of hosts, and the altar boy, Jeremy Malloy, took the cruets of wine and water.

The priest set the hosts on the altar and reached over and put the chalice in front of him. He removed the white linen cloth, or purificator, covering the chalice while Jeremy Malloy brought the cruet of water.

Father O'Malley held his fingers over the chalice and Jeremy poured water over them and returned the cruet to its place on the table beside the altar. The priest washed his fingers and wiped them on the purificator, then lowered his head and intoned a silent prayer. He opened the Bible beside him, held his hands above his head, and read aloud in his melodious, country brogue: "'Before he was given up to death, a death he freely accepted, he took bread and gave you thanks.'"

Father O'Malley picked up a host in both hands. "'Take this, all of you, and eat it; this is my body which will be given up for you.'"

His hands trembled as he raised the host, and his eyes darted to the congregation. When the priest laid down the communion wafer, the altar boy approached with the cruet of wine. Father O'Malley held out the chalice and Jeremy emptied the wine into it.

Holding the chalice aloft, he said, "'This is the cup of my blood ...'" He took a deep breath and his voice trembled as he finished the prayer. "'It will be shed for you and for all men so that sins may be forgiven.'"

The priest raised the cup to his mouth and stared down into its recesses. The deep purple of the wine—now changed to blood—shone in the bottom of the golden chalice. Father O'Malley put the cup to his lips and turned it up, the cold rim of the chalice burning his lips as the musky aroma of the wine crept up his nostrils.

After filling the chalice with hosts, he made his way to the altar rail with Jeremy Malloy beside him. Father O'Malley held the host at eye-level in front of Liam Flynn, the oldest member of the parish who stood stooped over, first in line for Communion. Liam refused to take the host in his hand, as the young people did, but instead stuck his tongue out and the priest placed the host in Liam's mouth.

Breda Slattery, one of the pillars of the church and founder of the Legion of Mary, stood behind Flynn. The priest felt lightheaded as he handed the host to Mrs. Slattery, who took it in her hands and placed it reverently into her mouth.

Nigel Greene, a visitor from England who remained seated during Communion, stood and let Mrs. Slattery pass in to her seat.

The Widow Kathleen Conlon in white veil and gloves, who sat beside her learning-disabled son, approached the altar and put her tongue out to receive

Communion. Father O'Malley placed the host gently on her tongue. "Body of Christ," he murmured, his mouth dry. A throbbing had begun at the back of his skull and his knees shook. Kathleen Conlon made the Sign of the Cross and returned to her seat, bumping the Communion table as she climbed into the pew beside her grown son, Desmond, who stared blankly at his hands.

Peggy Malloy, the altar boy's mother and the only woman in Ballycara with a ring pierced through her nose, approached the altar rail. The priest reached out the host to Peggy. He felt dizzy as she took the host on her tongue, blessed herself, and returned to her seat.

Seamus Larkin, the pubkeeper of the village and a big, muscular man, took Communion next, followed by James Roche, a pale, sickly looking man who had been in the village only a short time. A wave of nausea passed over Father O'Malley as he placed the host in Roche's outstretched palm, and beads of sweat formed on the priest's forehead.

Pain stabbed Father O'Malley's chest and his heart thundered. Disoriented, he glanced over at the altar boy, who gave him a questioning look.

The priest turned carefully to the altar and moved toward it as if intoxicated. His shoes felt heavy as concrete as he stepped behind the altar, placed the square of cardboard covered with linen—the pall—over the chalice, and put it away. He took in shallow, rapid breaths and a tremor ran through his body as he hastened to end Mass.

He held his right hand aloft and blessed the congregation. "The Mass is ended," he began, then stopped and craned his neck. A crow screeched outside the church, and the sound mesmerized him.

"Father," Jeremy Malloy whispered, tugging gently on the priest's chasuble.

Father O'Malley looked down at the boy mouthing words to him. Sweat ran down the priest's forehead and he reached up to wipe his brow. His skin felt clammy. He licked his lips.

This time the boy said louder to the priest, "'Go in peace ...'"

Father O'Malley's attention snapped back to the Mass. He realized at that moment, when Jeremy Malloy corrected *him*, that something was very wrong. He finished making the Sign of the Cross in the air and repeated, "The Mass is ended. Go in peace to love and serve the Lord."

In the sacristy Father O'Malley's head swam. He steadied himself on the counter in front of his dressing mirror and loosened the cincture around his waist.

"I'm going now, Father," said Jeremy. He had already shed his altar clothing and was set to dash out.

Father O'Malley looked at him and thought, *Don't leave me, child*. Sweat dripped from the priest's chin and a deep chill racked his body from the frozen tips of his toes to his head. He tried to work his mouth to beg the boy to stay, but it was as though a vast distance separated his thoughts from the mechanism that moved his jaws. He managed only the slightest squeak, which the boy took for a goodbye, and Jeremy Malloy raced out the door.

After removing the red stole from around his neck, the priest stood dazed in front of his dressing table for a long time. Then, in the mirror, he saw one of his congregation enter. He tried to turn, grateful that someone had come, but his body no longer responded to his will.

A hand pressed his shoulder from behind, fingers digging into his collarbone. Father O'Malley stood frozen, fighting the urge to collapse. He looked once at the hand on his shoulder as the pressure increased, and a fresh wave of nausea passed over him.

The priest felt the world go black.

ONE

Danny O'Flaherty looked up from Father O'Malley's handwritten letter, and peered out the bus window at the green fields of County Clare. He had left Dublin on Bus Eireaan in the darkness of early morning, but now the sun broke through a gray mass of clouds moving in from the Atlantic and cast rays of light on the hay bales stacked in the fields. In the distance, Danny saw a farmer and his helpers saving hay while the fine weather lasted, and a flock of crows screeched from the top of an ash tree in a graveyard beside the road. He glanced again at the letter in his hand.

"Sure, and how long are you over for?"

Danny turned to the elderly woman beside him who had not said a word since she got on at Newmarket on Fergus, near Shannon Airport, twenty minutes before. "Excuse me?"

"How long are you over for?"

Danny wondered how she had spotted him as a foreigner. It always startled him when they knew, even before he spoke, that he was American. Surely he didn't appear that different from the people around him?

After all, he was *Irish*-American and he had been living in Dublin for nearly a year. Maybe it was his clothes. He glanced down. A pair of new twill slacks, a sturdy pair of hiking boots, a leather flight jacket over his flannel shirt and a Donegal tweed cap. The jacket, maybe?

"Actually, I live in Dublin."

"Ah, that's grand!" said the woman. Her face was a nest of wrinkles and she worked her mouth nervously as if chewing something. "'Twould be your first trip to Clare, so?"

"No," he answered patiently, preparing for the usual barrage of questions he received when it became evident he was American. In fact, over the past year, Danny had spent weekends, holidays, and every other chance he got in the village of Ballycara, County Clare—the birthplace of Danny's grandfather—on the tip of the Loop Head Peninsula.

The woman gaped at him with open curiosity and seemed on the brink of further interrogation, but Danny, not in the mood for the usual grilling, turned to his own reflection in the window of the bus. Danny O'Flaherty had just turned forty-one and although flecks of silver speckled his black hair, his brown eyes had a youthful twinkle.

He had received Father O'Malley's letter the day after Irish schools let out for the summer. Although he spent as many of his weekends and holidays that he could in Ballycara, he had not been out to the village for nearly three weeks. He had been too busy preparing exams and final papers. Then, just yesterday, he received Father O'Malley's invitation to go fishing on the River Shannon after Sunday Mass. The priest had also disclosed in the letter that he had something he wanted to talk to Danny about, though he didn't say what it was.

This morning, Danny had hastened to the bus station for the trip to Ballycara.

Danny looked back at the priest's letter, then stole a quick glance at the woman peering over his shoulder, trying her best to see the contents of the letter. She glanced away, working her mouth nervously again.

Danny had two good reasons to go to Ballycara. First, to see his friend, Father O'Malley, and second to see Fidelma.

A couple of years ago, Danny had discovered that Fidelma Muldoon, the sacristan and housekeeper at the rectory of St. Bridget's Catholic Church in Ballycara, was a distant cousin, which Danny considered unfortunate since he had already fallen in love with her brilliant red hair and lilting brogue. He still wanted the relationship to be more than platonic and frequently invited her to visit him in Dublin. After all, they were not that closely related. But Fidelma remained against it.

"Sure, I hope you've no bad news," said the woman next to him.

Danny looked up absently. "Bad news?"

She tilted her head toward the letter in Danny's hand.

"Oh, that. No, of course not."

She worked her lips furiously and craned her neck toward the paper in Danny's hand.

"A friend of mine," Danny murmured, "the parish priest of Ballycara, has invited me to go fishing."

"Father O'Malley?"

"Yes," Danny said. "You know him?"

"Know of him. My name's Annie Finnarty. I live in Carrigaholt."

"Pleased to meet you."

"Where will you be staying in Ballycara?" she asked.

"With Mrs. Slattery. She still runs the Shannonside Bed and Breakfast."

"Sure, 'tis a lovely home."

"Mrs. Slattery's a lovely person."

"'Tis."

Danny looked down at the letter. He had agreed to meet Father O'Malley in Kilkee since the bus did not go as far as Carrigaholt, much less Ballycara. The priest wrote that he would pick Danny up on the main street where the bus let him off.

Outside it had begun to rain and the windows inside the bus steamed up. With his fist, Danny made a circle in the misty window. The bus stopped in the village of Cahermurphy and let two passengers off, then continued on in the rain—an almost glutinous mixture of mist and drizzle that cast an aura of gloom on the landscape. Even after a year in Dublin, Danny could still not get used to the changeable Irish weather.

"And what's your name, young man?" Mrs. Finnarty wanted to know.

"Danny O'Flaherty."

Her mouth worked thoughtfully for a moment. "Ah, yes. You're one of the O'Flahertys from Ballycara, sure. I remember now. Didn't you have something to do with finding that killer a couple years past? 'Twas a cousin of yours killed, I'm thinking."

Two years ago, Danny had discovered the murderer of his cousin Rose, and the truth about his Irish relations on his father's side. In the process he had fallen in love with the west of Ireland and had made many close friends in Ballycara, including Fidelma and Father O'Malley.

"That's right," Danny said, "cousin Rose."

When he reluctantly returned to New York after the death of cousin Rose, Danny had applied for a teacher exchange program with the hope of returning to County Clare. A week before school was to resume in New York, Danny learned he had been accepted into the program and that a spot had been found for him in Ireland. Unfortunately, he had not been assigned to a school in County Clare but rather to a rough inner-city school in the Ballymun section of Dublin.

Again, Danny gazed out the window at the passing scenery. The landscape changed as the bus drew closer to the coast: the trees and hedgerows stunted, the fields soggy. The villages here seemed worn and windswept, the façades of the buildings weathered from the sea air. Even though he had taken every opportunity—weekends, breaks, holy days—to come down to the Loop Head Peninsula, he never tired of the landscape. So different from Dublin it might have been another world—the Western World, as the Irish writer J.M. Synge called it.

Danny smiled at a sign beside the road: "Automatic Crossing. Drivers of large or slow vehicles or of herds of animals must phone before crossing." Did shepherds carry cell phones now?

"I hope the good father's gotten over that little problem of his," said the woman next to him.

"What?"

She peered over her half-lenses at him. "Father O'Malley has quite a reputation in the diocese."

Something about the way she said this bothered Danny. "What do you mean?"

"Now, I don't know anything about it, but Mrs. Rafferty told me she went to Midnight Mass one year in Ballycara and sure wasn't Father O'Malley drunk as a lord."

Danny glared at Annie Finnarty. "I don't believe that!"

"I didn't say I believed it, either," Mrs. Finnarty answered. "I said that's what Mrs. Rafferty said, and I've never known the woman to tell a lie."

Danny knew a lie when he heard one. After all, he knew Father O'Malley better than this old gossip. He was a good man and an excellent priest. He turned away from her, gazed out the window, and pondered all the time he had spent with Padraic O'Malley over the last year. Whether fishing or playing golf, or even at the horse races in Listowel, Danny could not remember the priest drinking to excess. Sure they'd had the odd jar together when Father O'Malley was in Dublin, and even been tipsy on a few occasions. But Danny couldn't picture the priest inebriated. Since Danny's father had died three years ago, he felt a strong attraction to the priest, and they had grown quite close in the last year. "I'm sure Mrs. Rafferty was imagining things," he said, half to himself, half to Annie Finnarty.

In Milltown Malbay, the end of the line for Bus Eireaan, all the passengers disembarked. Ongoing passengers would ride a school bus to the outlying villages, a fact that Danny had been unaware of his first trip down from Dublin.

"You've to take the bus," the driver had told Danny when he had failed to get off with the others, pronouncing bus so that it rhymed with goose.

"I'm on the *boose,*" Danny had shot back.

"For the children," the driver had said, leading Danny down the steps and pointing to a school bus loading children across the street.

"That?" Danny had asked.

"To Kilkee, sure."

He still felt foolish stepping up on the bus with a pack of nine- and ten-year-olds. He walked sheepishly past the driver, who smiled and waved good-naturedly as Danny found a seat in the back. The seats were small and cramped and he sat down next to a little carrot-haired fellow with thick glasses. Danny pulled his knees up, but they still rested awkwardly against the seat in front of him. He rested his right arm against the window, leaving hardly any room for his left.

Carrot-top had his face buried in a book. He looked up at Danny as if out of a thick fog as he adjusted his over-sized glasses and stared at Danny curiously. "Kilkee?" he asked.

"Kilkee," Danny answered. "You don't go to school on Sunday, do you?"

"Field trip," the boy groaned.

The three boys in the seat in front of him swung around and chorused, "You a Yank?"

"Right," Danny answered, "a Yank. But I live in Dublin."

"Ah, Dublin," one of the kids said as if it were as distant as Hong Kong. "'Tis a holiday you're having?"

"Not exactly."

"What then?" they asked.

Danny lowered his voice and the boys in front of him bent over the seat to hear. Even the kid next to him pulled his head up out of his book and turned toward Danny. Danny leaned forward. "I'm looking to catch the biggest brown trout in the west of Ireland."

The kids drew away. "Where?"

"The River Shannon."

"What kind of flies are you using?" they wanted to know.

"I'm not telling," Danny replied and winked.

The redhead next to Danny slammed his book shut and looked at Danny O'Flaherty in awe. "The biggest brown trout in the Shannon."

Danny smiled and patted the boy's head. Out the window the ice-blue Atlantic came suddenly into view. The bus raced down a narrow, potholed road that hugged the coast. The kids in the seat in front got off at Quilty, and the bus continued.

Danny closed his eyes and tried to nap despite his awkward position. He awoke as the bus pulled into the small seaside resort of Kilkee. The little redheaded fellow jumped up and raced off the bus. Several moments later Danny was able to coax his back into an upright position and he followed.

Victorian houses and shops painted pink, blue and yellow greeted him as he stepped from the bus. Kilkee, the closest major town to Ballycara, could only be considered major by Irish standards. Little more than an overgrown village, it attracted a smattering of Irish and German tourists each summer for its wide, sandy beach and the magnificent views of the nearby cliffs. The Stella Maris Hotel stood at one end of the main street along with a number of other accommodations— Lynch's B&B, Kincora House B&B, and the Bayview where Danny had stayed ever so briefly on his first trip to County Clare. At the foot of the street a wide shingle of sand faced Moore Bay. At each end of the beach precipitous cliffs plunged to the sea, and a stiff wind blew off the ocean, scattering candy wrappers and a paper cup across the narrow sidewalk.

The children who had ridden with Danny scattered like pigeons released from a cage and flew toward the security of their nests.

Danny lugged his fly rod, tackle box, and his bags onto the sidewalk, sat on his suitcase as the bus pulled away, and waited for Father O'Malley. Although it had stopped raining, the air was thick with humidity. He breathed in the bus' remaining diesel fumes and looked around, pleased to be back.

"Danny!"

He looked up, surprised by the female voice.

Fidelma Muldoon, her red hair trailing behind her, raced toward him from across the street.

Two

"What are you doing here?"

Fidelma flung her arms around Danny and held him, then stood back and searched his face with her green eyes. "Thank God you're here."

"What's wrong?" Surprised by her exuberant welcome, Danny pulled her into his arms again and buried his face in her fragrant hair. "I've missed you."

Fidelma Muldoon's fair skin contrasted with the abundance of bright red hair that poured from beneath her beige woolen tam. She wore a matching beige knit skirt and a high-necked, close-fitting white Aran tunic that hugged her breasts. Her forehead was lined with worry, and her normally dazzling green eyes were shuttered as if from fear. She gently pushed him away.

"Where's Father O'Malley?" he asked.

Fidelma pointed to the priest's red Nissan Micra across the street, and Danny picked up his bags and followed her. They stowed the baggage in the back of the car.

"Is something the matter?" he asked again.

"I hope not," Fidelma said.

"Where's Father O'Malley?"

"I'm not sure."

"Not sure?" Danny said, puzzled. "He was supposed to pick me up."

"I know."

"I see you have his car," Danny said, indicating the priest's Micra. "Is he back at the rectory?" Maybe he was getting his fishing gear ready and asked Fidelma to pick him up.

"Get in," said Fidelma, "and I'll tell you about it on the way."

"Tell me about what?"

In the car, Fidelma ground the starter several times before the engine caught. She popped the clutch, lurched onto the road, and sped out of Kilkee. "Father O'Malley didn't come back from Mass this morning."

"What?"

"He's been gone since nine-thirty."

Danny glanced at his watch: 5:30.

Just outside of town they picked up the Loop Head Drive. Danny buckled his seatbelt and noted the ancient, weather-beaten quality of the isolated farmhouses they passed, and the desolation of the landscape. "Oh, he probably forgot we were going fishing and went out for a few rounds of golf with one of the lads."

Unlike the countryside surrounding Dublin that he passed through on the bus, here mounds of earth, rather than stone fences, enclosed the fields, and canals crisscrossed the pastures. The narrow road had no shoulder since the earth was banked up to the edge of the road and covered with shrubbery. Out in a field, Danny saw a pile of broken furniture and wood.

"I don't think so." Fidelma downshifted and took a corner at what Danny considered excessive speed. "He would have taken the car."

The Nissan Micra handled well, however, and since it sat low to the ground, Danny thought it would be nearly impossible to flip. He sincerely hoped so. "I'm sure someone else picked him up."

"That's what's so queer. In fact," she explained, "it seems as though he never left the church at all."

"What do you mean?"

"It's as if he vanished."

A moment of silence passed before Danny said, "He didn't tell you he was going anywhere this morning?"

"No, and sure, I thought there was a good explanation why he didn't come home after Mass, and that he'd turn up later today."

"I can't believe anything's wrong, Fidelma. You know how absent-minded Father O'Malley can be. I'll bet he had a golf or dinner date and someone picked him up." Danny hesitated a moment. "He just forgot to tell you."

Fidelma reached out and touched Danny's hand. "I have a feeling something's happened."

Danny cleared his throat. "Why do you think that?"

Fidelma regarded him, her brow knitted over her green eyes. "Well," she began, "I got up to make Father's breakfast this morning before Mass. You know he always has his breakfast at the rectory afterward. He's very particular about having his meals served promptly."

Danny smiled, remembering the morning he and the priest had breakfast together in the rectory before setting off for the golf course in Kilkee. Father O'Malley insisted they have breakfast at nine o'clock sharp and was annoyed when Danny showed up five minutes late.

"So, I'd his breakfast ready after Mass. Sometimes he'll linger after church and talk to a few of the parishioners, so when he was late I didn't worry about it. But when he missed his breakfast and didn't come home for his lunch, I knew something was wrong."

Danny smiled again, remembering how much Father O'Malley enjoyed eating.

"It's not like him to miss a meal without at least letting me know. He's considerate that way. Besides, even if he is going out he always comes back to the rectory after Mass."

"I'm sure he left with someone else."

"That's what I thought. It's often he goes up for a few holes of golf in Kilkee, as you well know. But no one ever saw him leave the church after Mass." She shivered despite the coziness of the car. "And the most peculiar thing of all, Danny," she confided in a low voice, "is that he seems to have left wearing his vestments. When I went over to the sacristy, all I could find was Father's stole on the vanity table."

A lamb strayed onto the road and Fidelma jammed on the brakes as the car careened across the road, narrowly missing the lamb, and came to an abrupt halt.

Danny's hands shook as he reached out and touched Fidelma on the shoulder. "Are you all right?"

Fidelma took a shuddering breath and began to sniffle. "I'm going mad," she said, "worrying about Father O'Malley. Where is he?"

Danny got out and walked around to the driver's

side. "I'll drive," he said, opening Fidelma's door and helping her out. He led her to the passenger side. "You just sit here and relax."

He turned the car back onto the road and headed toward Ballycara. The mist had cleared and a sheet of gray nimbus clouds moved in from the Atlantic. Abandoned cottages stood derelict beside pastures of cattle and sheep enclosed by banks of earth. Danny saw another pile of broken pallets, old tires, and scraps of wood in a field beside the road. "What are all these piles of garbage?" Danny asked, pointing to the heap.

"Tomorrow's St. John's Day. Midsummer. The folks light bonfires all around the countryside."

Danny smiled. "Sounds pagan."

"Well, it was a Celtic celebration originally. Litha, I believe it was called. But it was renamed St. John's Day, in honor of St. John the Baptist."

"About this morning," he asked. "You didn't go to Mass yourself?"

"No. As I said, I was in the rectory preparing breakfast."

"You're sure no one saw him leave the church?" It would be hard to miss a priest in full regalia strolling down the street.

"I've asked everyone who was at church this morning. No one saw him leave. It makes my skin crawl. It's like he vanished into thin air."

"Did anyone see a car waiting for him?"

"No. No one saw anything out of the ordinary."

"But he had to leave the church, Fidelma."

Outside, mist licked the car windows and Danny

felt good to be out of the weather. But worry lines creased Fidelma's face and her lips seemed thin and drawn.

"Has anyone thought of a reason why Father O'Malley would not come home after Mass?" Danny asked.

"Haven't I racked my brain with that question all day, Danny, and still I can't answer it. All I can think ..."

"Yes?"

"Well, you'll say I'm daft."

"No! What?"

"Well, there's the curse, sure."

"What curse?"

"I'm certain Mrs. Slattery told you about it."

"Ah, yes. You mean that old legend about no good coming to the priests of St. Bridget's because the rectory was built in a direct line between two ring forts."

"That's right."

"You don't believe that nonsense, do you?"

"I don't know what to believe, Danny," Fidelma said, folding and unfolding her hands. "But haven't the last three priests come to a bad end? And now Father O'Malley has disappeared without a trace."

"Nobody's disappeared, Fidelma."

At Cross, they passed the old building where Danny's grandfather had gone to school. When they drove by the graveyard at Kilballyowen where his great-grandparents, Daniel and Mary O'Flaherty, were buried both Danny and Fidelma blessed themselves.

Fidelma smiled. "So, have you come back to the Church?"

"Well, I go a bit more frequently than I did. It's

something I still struggle with, you know. Once a Catholic always a Catholic."

"Sure, and they'll be making you a saint next."

"Knock it off, Fidelma."

Funny that with all the time Danny spent with Father O'Malley in the past year they rarely, if ever, discussed religion. Only once when they were playing nine holes at the course in Kilkee did Father O'Malley say, "We missed you at Mass this morning."

Danny had smiled sheepishy and replied, "Slept late," then missed an easy shot.

"It might improve your golf game," the priest had quipped, but he never raised the subject again.

Danny came to realize that perhaps one reason they had grown so close was that the priest related to Danny only as a person and not a parishioner, a distinction for which Danny was grateful. As the parish priest in a small village, Father O'Malley's status isolated him in many ways from his flock. Danny was a blow-in—an outsider—in whom Father O'Malley could easily confide. But what was it he had wanted to confide on their fishing trip? He had written in his letter that he wanted to talk to Danny about something.

Danny said to Fidelma, "There was a woman on the bus ..." He searched for a delicate way to put it. "... who suggested that Father O'Malley had a, uh, drinking problem."

Fidelma's emerald eyes caught fire and burned like green flame. "Who said that?"

"Just an old woman on the bus."

"From Ballycara?"

"No, from Carrigaholt."

"Well, that explains it. Sure Father O'Malley'd have the odd jar. You know that as well as I do. But I'd not call that a problem."

"No, I suppose not. I just asked." Danny lowered his voice. "I'm just looking for anything." He took a deep breath. "You don't think it's even remotely possible that he went on a drinking binge?"

Fidelma looked over at Danny. "Danny O'Flaherty, if you intend to do nothing but insult our parish priest, then as far as I'm concerned you can go straight back to Dublin!" Fidelma snatched her purse and made as if she were ready to jump out of the car.

"Wait, Fidelma." Danny reached out and took her arm. "I just asked so we can find out where Father O'Malley might have gone. If I can't ask a simple question, then I might just as well go straight back to Dublin. And you can go straight to—"

Fidelma looked at him and yanked her arm away, her eyes blazing. "Danny O'Flaherty, don't you dare—"

"I'm sorry, Fidelma." Danny ran his hand through his hair, thinking maybe he should slow down a bit. Yes, there were questions to ask, but he had time. "Now you've got *me* worried about Father O'Malley."

"Well, 'tis all right," Fidelma said grudgingly, patting his arm.

"Okay. Now, I'll only ask one more time." Danny absently fiddled with the gear shift. "Is it even remotely possible that Father O'Malley went on a drinking spree?"

Fidelma looked at him coldly. "I would say it is highly unlikely."

"Okay," Danny conceded. "Enough said."

Outside of Ballycara Danny and Fidelma spotted Desmond Conlon walking beside the road toward the village.

"Shall we give him a ride?" Danny asked as he downshifted and slowed the car.

Fidelma rolled down the window on her side and called to Desmond, "Will you take a lift, Desmond?"

Desmond Conlon said nothing as he walked toward the car and got into the back seat. He was well over six feet tall with wide square shoulders, a thick neck, black hair, and big calloused hands with red knuckles. No one knew exactly what had happened to Desmond as a child, but although he was twenty-five years old, he was not mentally capable of living on his own. He lived with his mother, the Widow Kathleen Conlon, and in spite of his handicap he was an expert mechanic and handyman, always in demand in Ballycara to do everything from carpentry work to fixing tractors. Although Desmond might walk out in the winter without a coat and hat on if his mother didn't remind him, he could take a tractor apart and put it back together again in a matter of hours.

"You haven't seen Father O'Malley today, have you Desmond?"

"At church."

"No, I mean after Mass."

Desmond shook his head.

The road climbed a steep grade and at the top afforded a magnificent view of the ocean, its creamy breakers crashing against the rocks at Loop Head, and the patchwork of farms that blanketed the hillsides to the cliffs. Coming around a bend, Danny could see the harbor of Carrigaholt in the distance and the ruins of O'Brien's Castle. Only three weeks ago, he and Father O'Malley had driven beyond that castle to fish the Shannon.

"Do you ever wonder," Danny had asked Father O'Malley as he flipped his fishing line out onto the water, "what you might have done if you had not become a priest?"

Father O'Malley had looked up, startled at first by the question. Then he seemed to grow pensive. "I might have married," the priest had said. "Had a family." But he would say no more, so Danny dropped the subject.

He scanned the water's edge as they passed, hoping for a glimpse of the priest's familiar profile. He wondered about what might have happened to his friend. Maybe he had fallen into the Shannon while fishing alone, or had had a heart attack while out walking on the beach, and been swept away by the tide. Danny shuddered and glanced at his watch. It was almost six o'clock.

The road passed through the center of a collection of weather-beaten houses, each with a chimney at either end. Desmond Conlon got out without a word in front of Carmody's Grocery Shop, its paint chipped and faded like the façades of most of the houses, although one had been painted a bright pink since Danny's last visit. The street was deserted, except for a Collie that nosed around the side of a building, then lifted its leg against the wall. Seamus Larkin had a fancy new neon Guinness sign in the window of Larkin's Pub, but other than that the village looked the same. At the end of the street stood Mrs. Slattery's bright green house, Shannonside, with its mustard-colored trim.

"Shall we stop at Shannonside?" Fidelma asked.

"No," said Danny. "Let's go see if Father O'Malley's back at the rectory yet. I'll bet you five pounds he's waiting for us when we get there."

"I hope you win the bet," said Fidelma.

Three

St. Bridget's Catholic Church, built in 1908 in the Gothic style, towered over the main street of Ballycara flanked by a graveyard shaded by a grove of poplars. Across from the crumbling headstones and Celtic crosses sat the parish rectory, a modern dormer bungalow with a pitched slate roof.

Danny parked the car beside the rectory and handed the keys to Fidelma. She ran inside to check on Father O'Malley and returned looking crestfallen. "He isn't there."

"Let's go have a look around the church," Danny said as he got out of the car.

They strolled in the cool air toward the church. When Danny and Fidelma reached the bottom of the hill, they turned into the churchyard and walked across the grass. Although a few crows screeched in the poplar trees, the early evening was still, punctuated occasionally by the cry of a seagull.

Danny opened the squeaking doors of the church and he and Fidelma entered the chilly sanctuary. A row of candles beneath the statue of St. Bridget glittered in the darkness, and three stained-glass windows above the altar let in a faint light.

Danny dabbed his fingers in the basin of holy water, blessed himself, and walked up the aisle past the stations of the cross hanging on the walls, his footfalls resounding in the gloom, until he paused before the altar. To the right, a wooden door led to the sacristy, and above the door stood a statue of St. Joseph. The air smelled of candle wax and incense.

How many years had it been since he'd felt the purifying feeling of elation he knew as a child after taking Communion and returning to his seat to say his prayers, or after going to confession and scrubbing his soul clean? In some ways Danny blamed the reforms of Vatican II for his departure from the Church. After the Mass had changed from Latin to English, and the priest no longer performed the rituals of the water and wine with his back to the congregation but faced it openly, the mystery of the Mass had finally been dispelled for Danny, and had lost its allure.

But Danny knew that he was rationalizing his loss of faith. There simply came a time as a teenager when he could no longer focus his attention on the Mass. At first he felt guilty for it, but then even the guilt began to subside and his mind wandered throughout Mass.

Ironically, it was the nuns—who had challenged him to think deeply about his faith—who had inadvertently turned him against the Church. Because ultimately he could not accept the notion of bread and wine being turned into the actual body and blood of Christ. So he drifted from the Church, or from its doctrines at least. Yet, in the litany of forms that he filled out in his journey through life, in the space that asked for religion, he always wrote: Roman Catholic.

Then, since moving to Dublin, he had found himself drawn slowly back to the Church. He attended Mass more frequently than he ever had in New York. Maybe the stories he had heard on the Loop Head Peninsula, about the times of the Penal Laws when Catholics had been forbidden to own property or practice their religion, had nudged him back to Mass. Many times Danny visited *An Cillan*, at the tip of Loop Head, the Church of the Little Ark—commemorating a time when Mass was celebrated on a homemade altar, or ark, that was set up offshore during low tide, outside the jurisdiction of the government. If his forebears had suffered so much to hold onto their faith, who was he to toss it out the window?

A floorboard squeaked near the rear of the church and Danny's pulse quickened. He grabbed the altar rail, then turned and peered intently into the darkness, trying to detect the origin of the noise. But he could not. He stole along the altar rail toward the side door where Fidelma waited for him. They entered the sacristy and Fidelma clicked on the lights. Danny examined the sacristy for a few minutes, opened a cupboard door, riffled through a drawer. He stepped into the priest's large walk-in closet and searched through his vestments, but found nothing of interest.

Danny turned slowly in a circle, staring at the walls. "If he didn't leave through the sacristy door, then he had to leave some other way."

"I don't see how."

"The window?"

"Painted shut. Desmond Conlon's doing, I'm thinking, though sure he's never admitted it."

At the back of the sacristy, Danny's gaze fell on a hatch flush with the floor like a trap door. He pointed. "What's that?"

"That goes to the basement, sure."

"Help me move this stuff," Danny said, as he shoved a box of Mass booklets aside.

Fidelma pulled the box of booklets away and moved aside another box of outdated missals.

Danny grabbed the handle of the hatch and gave it a pull, but it held fast, locked with a padlock. "Do you have the key to this?"

"I don't believe I've ever been in the basement."

"Where does Father O'Malley keep his keys?"

"On a loop he wears on his belt." Fidelma touched her waist. "He has a leather strap on his belt with keys to the church, the rectory, the basement."

"Where is it?"

"Sure, it's on his waist. He never goes anywhere without it."

"Do you have another set?"

"Down at the rectory. But I'm sure he wouldn't go down there. Nothing but a bunch of old dusty junk."

"Let's get the key."

When Fidelma came back with the second set of keys, Danny tried the first three without success. With the fourth key, the lock clicked open and Danny grasped the handle on the door. He realized his hands were shaking.

"Do you have a flashlight?" he asked hoarsely.

Fidelma fetched a flashlight from a drawer and handed it to him.

He swung open the door of the basement and looked back at Fidelma. "You want to wait here while I look around?" he asked.

But she didn't move.

"I'll only be a minute."

Fidelma frowned in annoyance, then she turned and walked out of the sacristy.

The wooden stairs groaned as Danny descended into the darkness. He played the flashlight's beam over the dusty interior of the cellar and the usual junk one would expect to find in a church basement. Along one wall were stacks of lumber and assorted building materials left over from some renovation project on the church. Along another wall were boxes stacked from floor to halfway up the wall as well as red plastic bags of coal and turf for the furnace.

Danny stepped over a pile of bricks and flicked the light around the interior. A peculiar odor emanated from a dark corner and Danny pointed the beam in that direction. He saw a mound of something spread out on the floor, and at first he thought it was a pile of turf.

When his brain at last made sense of what his eyes saw, the pounding in his chest became a roaring in his ears. He felt bile rise in his throat as the smell became more prominent.

Father O'Malley lay on his back on the floor in the corner, neatly arranged with his hands crossed over his chest, still wearing his vestments. The tip of his tongue protruded through his lips and his eyes bulged slightly. It looked as though he had descended the stairs after Mass, lay down in the far corner of the cellar and died.

When Danny approached, he saw a green fly crawl out of one of the priest's nostrils. The flesh on Father O'Malley's face was waxy and taut; his lips pale.

"Oh, God, no," Danny gasped. He stepped forward and stood over the body, then fell to his knees beside the priest and felt for a pulse on Father O'Malley's neck. His skin was purplish and his forefinger left a white mark where he placed it below the jaw. Danny felt no pulse. He turned his head, covered his mouth with his hand, and gagged.

He had seen corpses before and the sight had never revolted him. But this ... What had happened? Another wave of nausea passed over Danny, and he turned away again, the bitter taste of bile burning his throat. He swallowed with difficulty and turned back to the corpse, his eyes filled with tears. "What in God's name happened?" he said aloud as if speaking to the priest.

Already the lower jaw and neck had stiffened, yet the body lay in a peaceful repose, still clothed in cassock and surplice. Then Danny noticed something that almost drove out the horror and revulsion. In his hands, Father O'Malley held a set of rosary beads. His right thumb marked the beginning of the second decade. His fingernails looked waxy, almost translucent.

Danny's legs trembled as he climbed the stairs, and walked through the sacristy into the church.

Fidelma glanced up. "What's wrong?"

"Go get Kelley," he said gently, tears running down his cheeks.

"What is it?"

Danny let his head fall. "He's down there."

Fidelma fled from the church.

"Good God in Heaven, now what?" said Garda Kelley as he joined Danny outside the sacristy with Fidelma beside him. "I'm on my way to the airport." Kelley pointed to the car where his gray-haired wife sat patiently waiting, the backseat piled with suitcases.

Danny avoided Fidelma's eyes as he spoke to the garda. "Down in the basement."

"Let's have a gander."

Garda Kelley followed Danny down the stairs, past the piles of bricks and building materials, to the far end of the cellar.

He shone a beam on the dead priest's face, illuminating the waxy pallor of Father O'Malley's sallow skin. A speck of blood had dried below his left nostril. "My God!"

Kelley photographed the corpse with a cheap instamatic with flash, and scribbled in his notebook. Father O'Malley's black curly hair was neatly brushed, unmolested.

It was as though the priest had been laid out and sacrificed with an invisible weapon that left no wounds, like an offering to some perverse god.

"I'll have Fidelma bring the ambulance," said Kelley. He walked halfway up the stairs and called to her.

"Are you sure you want him moved?" Danny asked as he paced around the area of the corpse trying to figure out the odd scene. Why did he come down here after Mass? Did he have a heart attack?

Danny glanced up at Kelley, whose head stuck out of the cellar, then knelt beside the priest, reached beneath his cassock, and ran his hands around the priest's waist, feeling for the ring of keys.

"Don't touch anything," Kelley said as he came back down the stairs.

Danny stood. There were no keys on Father O'Malley's belt.

"Dr. Cassidy will have to sign the death certificate," Kelley said absently.

Within half an hour, two young men in white smocks appeared at the door of the basement. Danny and Garda Kelley moved out of the way as they lowered a gurney down the stairs.

"May the Lord have mercy on him," said the older of the two as he hefted his end of the gurney.

The men carefully put the body on the gurney and covered the priest with a white sheet. Danny stood back with his flashlight lowered. The glow from the light threw a strange pall over the scene. Garda Kelley replaced his pen and notebook in his top pocket and blessed himself as the attendants hauled the gurney up the staircase. Danny stood bewildered, playing his light over the place where the body had lain.

"The dear man," said Kelley.

"Yes," said Danny absently. "What do you think happened?"

"Looks like he went to get something down here after Mass and had a stroke or a heart attack."

"But the basement was locked."

"Sure, and he had a key."

"I mean it was locked when I got here. Someone locked the basement after Father O'Malley went down here."

"Shall we go up?" said Kelley, ignoring Danny's concern.

Outside the sacristy, Fidelma stared at the ambulance as it pulled away. Danny put his arm around her and Kelley turned away as she buried her face in Danny's chest.

Garda Kelley cleared his throat and Danny turned to him, releasing Fidelma. "I think there needs to be a postmortem," Danny said.

"O'Flaherty," Kelley grunted, "do you intend to tell me how to do my job?"

"Of course not."

"I told you Dr. Cassidy will sign the death certificate. I have a flight to catch in Shannon."

"Then I may call the State Pathologist myself," said Danny. "I don't think Father O'Malley died of any heart attack."

"Mr. O'Flaherty," said Kelley, "do not presume that you are in any way involved in the investigation of this unfortunate event."

"Event?"

"I've no idea what you're thinking. But there did not appear to be the least bit of a struggle evident. Father O'Malley was not in the best of health. Dr. Cassidy will attest to that."

"But the basement door had been locked after him."

"I'm sure Fidelma locked the basement."

"I did not," she said.

"Probably the altar boy, then. But, no matter. I'm leaving for Ibiza. I have not had a vacation in ten years and I will not disappoint my wife now. Leave this to the Garda Siochana." He handed Danny a business card. "If you have a complaint about the way this is being handled you can contact Chief Superintendent of the Clare division, Lawrence Burke, in Ennis. But I really don't see what business it is of yours."

"Danny's the one who found him," Fidelma said. Tears squeezed from the corners of her eyes. "If he hadn't come down here from Dublin we may have never known what happened to Father O'Malley."

"I would not be so sure of that, Fidelma." Kelley rocked on his heels and toes. "I'm as sorry about Father O'Malley as you are. But it's clear he had a stroke or a heart attack. Don't make this out to be something it's not."

"I want to know what happened," Fidelma muttered.

"He has gone on to his reward in heaven," said Kelley. "As I've said, leave it to the Garda Siochana."

"The guards." Fidelma's voice rose angrily. "That's what you said when Danny's cousin Rose was murdered."

Kelley glared at Fidelma as if she were a naughty child. "No one's been murdered. There's no evidence that a crime's been committed here a-tall."

Danny knew that Kelley's ego still smarted from his failure to solve the murder of Danny's cousin, Rose O'Flaherty Noonan, and the garda remained angry with Danny for beating him to the catch. Now he just seemed anxious to get on to his vacation.

"And," Fidelma continued, "if it hadn't been for Danny, we'd not have known what happened then, either."

"Fidelma," Danny said quietly, pulling her back into his arms. "Let it go."

"I'll *not* let it go," she said, pushing him away. "I want to know what happened to Father ..." but she could not finish.

Garda Kelley opened the door of his green Volkswagen Golf, parked beside the sacristy. "Can you drive, Dear," he said to his wife, "while I write my report. We'll fax it to Superintendent Burke from the airport."

Fidelma held onto Danny as if she were drowning.

"I'll call Dr. Cassidy and have him fill out the death certificate," Kelley said to no one in particular, as his wife started the engine. She put the car in gear and rolled forward.

The garda stuck his head out the passenger side. "I'm warning you, O'Flaherty," said Garda Kelley. "Let the Irish garda take care of Irish business."

Four

After Kelley drove away, Fidelma took Danny down to Shannonside in the car, both of them stunned. Finally, Danny said, "I can't believe this. It doesn't seem real."

Fidelma wiped her eyes with a tissue and shook her head.

"Did Father O'Malley wear his keys on his belt even at Mass?"

"He did," Fidelma said, sniffling. "Under his cassock."

"They weren't on him downstairs in the basement. I checked."

Fidelma stared at him. "They weren't?"

"No. Who else had access to the keys to the basement?"

"Just me. Only Father O'Malley and I have a set. Oh," Fidelma added, "Peggy Malloy stored a few boxes down there last year before they got settled into their home."

"She had a key?"

"For a while. I loaned her mine. But she gave it back, sure."

"Who else had access to the basement?"

"Well, from time to time, quite a few people go into the basement. Liam Flynn sells his turf to the church to burn in the furnace. Seamus sells soft drinks for the youth dances and I've loaned him a key to put them in the basement. Even Brendan has helped Liam bring bags of turf down there. Why? What are you thinking?"

"Nothing."

As usual, Mrs. Slattery worked in the garden beside the house. She carried a hand sprayer and squirted weed killer between the rows of potatoes while Desmond Conlon pulled weeds from between the plants. Mrs. Slattery lifted her wrinkled face when she saw the Micra pull up, waved, and walked stoop-shouldered toward the car. "Danny O'Flaherty," she called, "you're back again."

When Danny got out of the car, the gusts of wind blowing off the sea nearly toppled him, but he steadied himself and embraced the old woman. Neither Danny nor Fidelma spoke to Mrs. Slattery of what they had just found.

"So, how long are you here for this time?" asked Mrs. Slattery as she handed the herbicide sprayer to Desmond, who continued where she left off.

"Well, schools in Dublin are over for the year." Danny turned to Fidelma for help. He was not sure how to break the news. "Mrs. Slattery, I'm afraid—" he began.

Suddenly, Fidelma said, "I need to get back to the rectory."

"Won't you come in for tea," Mrs. Slattery asked her, "while I get Danny settled in?"

Fidelma glanced at Danny. "I don't think so."

"Are you sure, Fidelma?" asked Mrs. Slattery, looking at her curiously. "Is something wrong?"

Fidelma turned to Danny and said, "I have to go. I have calls to make." She gave him a peck on the cheek. "Thanks, Danny."

"Come on with ye," interrupted Mrs. Slattery. "Ye'll have plenty of time to gab later." She reached into the pocket of her housedress and handed Desmond Conlon a ten pound note. "When you finish the weeds, Desmond, run along home to your mother. And will you bring back that bottle of herbicide she borrowed. We're running low."

Inside, a turf fire glowed in the fireplace and Danny inhaled the aroma of lamb stew simmering in the kitchen. He set his bags down in the parlor and took stock of the changes that had been made to the house. Mrs. Slattery had just begun the renovations to Shannonside three weeks ago and it amazed him to see how much was finished. The interior had been given a fresh coat of pale yellow paint and a new painting (hunters on horseback chasing a fox over a stone fence) had been placed on one wall. A new oriental rug in front of the fireplace and vases of flowers on the wide window sills brightened the living room.

"Mrs. Slattery ..." Danny began again.

"Would you sign the guest registry, please," she said.

"Guest registry?"

Mrs. Slattery beamed. "Sure, haven't I earned the seal of *Bord Failte*? Shannonside is now a member of the Town and Country Homes Association. I'd to be approved by an inspector from *Bord Failte*, don't you know."

"Congratulations." Danny felt a twinge of nostalgia for the shabby gentility of his previous visits. "But I really need to tell you something."

"And," Mrs. Slattery added, taking a colorful guidebook down from the mantel. "I'm in the nineteen ninety-nine Guest Accommodation Booklet."

Danny examined the book: "Official *Bord Failte*—Irish Tourist Board Guide for all registered hotels, guesthouses, holiday centres, holiday hostels, listed town and country homes and farmhouses—setting out maximum charges."

Danny felt disoriented, as if he had never found the dead priest at all. "Listen, I have to tell you—"

"And I've three other rooms let today beside your own. Two of them are en-suite."

"In what?"

"En-suite—full bathroom in the room."

On his previous visits, though Danny had paid for his room, he never really thought of it as a bed & breakfast, simply as Mrs. Slattery's home. He'd had it to himself most times. "You have three other guests?"

"Six guests, actually." Mrs. Slattery smiled. "And that nice Mr. Greene just yesterday helped me put new wallpaper in the bathroom upstairs. You'll meet them all at tea, sure. Now, the guest registry, please."

Danny signed the registry and perused the list of guests who had stayed at Shannonside in the last week. There had been a few guests from England as well as from the Continent, mostly France and Germany. Only one other North-American beside Danny had ever stayed with Mrs. Slattery, a couple from Toronto, Canada, also named O'Flaherty. Interesting, Danny thought. Distant cousins, perhaps, digging up their roots?

Currently staying at Shannonside were Mr. James Roche, Ballycara; Monsieur and Madame Marcel Gilbert of St. Malo, France, with one child, Gisselle; and Mr. and Mrs. Nigel Greene of Birmingham, England.

Mrs. Slattery looked over Danny's shoulder at her guest book. "Shall I show you your room, so?" She pointed upstairs.

"I'm afraid I have some bad news," Danny said, feeling suddenly tired.

For the first time since he got to the B&B, Mrs. Slattery was silent. "Bad news?" she asked at last.

"I think maybe you should sit down." Danny pulled the chair from under the table where the guest registry sat and helped Mrs. Slattery into it.

"Well, what is it?"

"Fidelma and I just found Father O'Malley."

Mrs. Slattery clapped her hands. "That's grand. Where was the old rascal hiding?"

"He's dead," Danny whispered. "We found him in the basement of the church."

"Dead?" Mrs. Slattery's smile collapsed. "Jesus, Mary and Joseph pray for us! What happened?"

"I'm not sure. Kelley thinks he had a stroke or a heart attack."

"Oh, Lord in Heaven, no." Mrs. Slattery buried her face in her hands. Her body shook with spasms of grief as Danny put his hand awkwardly on her shoulder. Finally, she looked up, wiped her eyes with the back of her hand, blessed herself and said, "I'll show you to your room."

"Can I use the telephone first?" Danny asked, taking the card Garda Kelley had given him from his wallet.

"You know where it is."

Danny finally got the home number of Chief Superintendent Lawrence Burke, commander of the Clare division. The garda listened patiently as Danny introduced himself.

"Ah, yes. I remember you," the policeman said. "Fine job you did on the Rose Noonan case."

"Thanks."

"As every guard knows, the cooperation of the public is our greatest asset in solving crimes."

"I appreciate that."

"However," the Chief Superintendent went on, "Kelley called me from the airport. I see no reason to suspect foul play in Father O'Malley's death. It looks like an open and shut case."

"But an autopsy would dispel any doubts."

"According to Kelley, there are no doubts to dispel. We don't know the exact cause of Father O'Malley's death, but there's no reason to suspect homicide."

"But the basement door was locked after him."

"Kelley seems to think the sacristan locked up afterwards."

"She said she didn't."

"Let me tell you something about witnesses, Danny," Burke went on pleasantly. "If five people are standing on a street corner and a green car goes by, when you ask the witnesses to describe the color of the car, each one of them will swear it was a different color. None of them is lying, yet they're absolutely convinced they remember what color the car was."

"I have a bad feeling about this thing," Danny said.

"Sure you do. I understand the priest was a good friend of yours."

"I think there should be a postmortem."

"I'm not against it," Burke said. "But I doubt the bishop would go for it. You know, it is only recently that the Catholic Church even allows cremation of a body. I don't think the bishop would care to see Father O'Malley's remains dissected because someone has a bad feeling about his death."

Danny said nothing.

"I've got to go, Mr. O'Flaherty," Superintendent Burke said politely. "Keep in touch."

Danny hung up the phone and followed Mrs. Slattery up the stairs to his room. He hung his shirts and jacket in the old wooden wardrobe beside the door and stowed his suitcase under the bed.

Danny unlaced his boots and rubbed his temples, lay down on the bed, and dropped off to sleep.

He awoke to a loud knocking at the door. "Supper," Mrs. Slattery called.

Must have dozed off, he thought, rubbing his eyes and getting up from the bed, feeling groggy. He checked his watch: eight o'clock.

Six people sat at the dining room table when Danny came down. Mrs. Slattery introduced the French couple, Monica and Marcel, and their daughter, Gisselle, a tow-headed youngster of about nine or ten.

"And this is Nigel and Eleanor Greene," Mrs. Slattery continued the introductions, "of Birmingham, England."

"Pleased to meet you." Danny shook hands all around. "Where's Mr. Roche?" He had seen the name in the guest book.

"He won't be joining us," said Mrs. Slattery. "Shall we say grace? In the name of the Father, and of the Son, and of the Holy Spirit."

Everyone blessed themselves but the English couple, who bowed their heads as Mrs. Slattery said grace. At the end of grace, Mrs. Slattery added a special prayer for the repose of the soul of Father O'Malley, then scooped lamb stew from the pot in the center of the table and served Danny first. He waited until everyone was served, then dug into the stew, thick with potatoes, carrots, and chunks of lamb.

"So," began Nigel Greene, "have you heard the one about the three-legged pig?"

"Nigel, please," whined Eleanor Greene, "not tonight. Have some respect for the dead."

"Be a sport, darling. Everybody needs cheering up. Especially at a time like this. Besides, I'm sure they haven't heard it."

"Nigel ..." Eleanor Greene wore a pained expression; the sign of a woman bound to a tedious husband. "Please. The parish priest was just found dead!"

"You see," Nigel began, oblivious to his wife's complaints and to her better sense, "chap from London goes on holiday in Ireland and meets a farmer."

"Oh, for goodness' sake, Dear," his wife mumbled, pouring herself a cup of tea.

Nigel plowed on, but his telling seemed forced. "While the chap's talking to the farmer a pig comes up. Chap notices the pig only has three legs. Says to the farmer, 'Excuse me, sir, but your pig only has three legs.' Farmer says, 'I know; that's my favorite pet. This pig has saved my life many times. One time the house caught fire. She ran in and pulled the blankets off me bed. It was so cold I woke up. Then the pig ran into the children's room squealing and squealing and pulled the covers off the beds. We all ran out of the house and the house burned down but nobody got hurt.'"

Danny caught himself drumming the table with his fingers. Greene had an annoying accent and he mimicked perfectly the Irish farmer in the story. How could this clown sit here telling jokes, Danny thought bitterly, after a body had just been found under his own nose? Danny thought again of Father O'Malley, and a wave of sadness passed over him.

The French couple's faces were twisted into expressions of extreme concentration as they tried to follow the unfamiliar language. Mrs. Greene pointedly studied the painting across the room. God knows how many times she has sat through this one, Danny thought. Only the French child and Mrs. Slattery seemed interested and their eyes were riveted to Greene's face.

"So the chap from London asks, 'Did the pig lose

its leg in the fire?' 'Not a bit of it,' the Irishman said. 'Then there was another time I was out in the field cutting hay and the tractor flipped over and sure didn't it land on me leg. Well, the pig went to my car, got the jack out of the boot of the car, came back out to the field, jacked the tractor up, and I was able to get me leg out from under it.'"

Eleanor Greene let out an almost imperceptible sound, a cross between a sigh and a moan, and absently stirred her stew.

The French couple, thinking the joke was over, politely smiled and nodded, but their smiles dropped as Nigel Greene plunged on toward the punchline. "Chap from London asks, 'Well how did it lose its leg doing that?' The Irishman answers: 'Sure, he didn't lose his leg like that. Man, you wouldn't want to eat a good pig like that all at one time would you?'"

There was a moment of silence in the dining room and then Mrs. Greene mumbled, "Oh, dear," and clicked her tongue as Nigel roared with laughter. Mrs. Slattery chuckled, and the French couple looked at each other. The child leaned over and began rapidly interpreting the joke into French for them and Danny looked at Nigel Greene with hatred, and at his wife with sympathy.

"Isn't that a good one?" Nigel Greene said to Danny enthusiastically, putting on an exaggerated brogue, "'you can't eat a pig like that all at one time.' Get it? The farmer was eating the pig slowly, one leg at a time, because it was his favorite."

"I'm sure they *get* it," his wife put in icily, pursing her lips.

"Clever," said Mrs. Slattery.

"Have you heard the one about the Italian, the Jew, and the Irishman?" Nigel began again.

"Please, Nigel," Eleanor implored, "for my sake," then deftly changed the subject. "So, what brings you to Ireland?" She was looking at Danny.

"I'm on a teacher exchange program in Dublin."

"Oh, really? How interesting."

It seemed like everyone was trying to avoid talking about Father O'Malley.

Suddenly, the French couple burst out giggling, having heard the pig joke retold in French, and they nodded appreciatively toward Nigel, who beamed.

"Wouldn't want to eat a good pig like that all at one time," Nigel yelled to them as if they were hard of hearing.

Finally, Danny couldn't take it anymore. "I don't know why we're sitting here joking. Father O'Malley is dead. He was the best friend I had in Ballycara." Danny's voice cracked. "I'm going to miss him."

"We're all going to miss him, Danny," said Mrs. Slattery. "But, you know, there hasn't been an ounce of luck in that rectory since it was built."

"What do you mean?" Eleanor asked.

Mrs. Slattery launched into the same tale Danny had heard from Tim Mahoney and Fidelma. But this time he listened with acute interest.

"You see, the rectory was built thirteen years ago. Well, the first priest who moved into that house was there about a fortnight and he died. No one could explain it. He wasn't the least bit sick. Another priest came. He said one first Friday Mass and sure didn't he die as well. Then, the third priest came and he went up to Galway to pick up some statues he'd ordered from Italy. On the way home from Galway he ran into a lorry and was killed. But he didn't die until the eighth of December."

"The Feast of the Immaculate Conception," said Nigel Greene.

"That's right, and sure all the people then said they should never have built the rectory where they did. You see it's in a direct line between one ring fort and another one about a quarter of a mile away."

"What's a ring fort?" the French girl asked.

"It's a circle of stones left behind by the people who lived in Ireland hundreds of years ago. Some of the old folks believe that the fairies move up and down there. You see, they have a pathway between the two forts. And the rectory sits square in the middle of the path. I'm telling you I've been expecting something dreadful to happen. There'll never be an ounce of luck in that house. I might be just an old countrywoman, but I know this much, you don't disturb the ring forts."

"Nonsense," said Nigel Greene. "Bunch of old *pisoigs.*"

"Bunch of what?" Danny asked.

"Old folk stories," Mrs. Slattery snapped. "Well, you might think 'tis, but that's not likely to help Father O'Malley, sure."

"How long has Father O'Malley been in this parish?" Eleanor Greene asked.

She thought a moment. "'Twould be three years next February."

"Yet nothing happened to him all this time," Mrs. Greene responded.

"Sure, the fairies have their own sense of time," Mrs. Slattery said, raising her teacup to her lips.

Danny had a lot of questions for Mrs. Slattery, but he preferred to speak to her privately. "How long have you been in Ballycara?" Danny asked the French couple.

Their daughter spoke to her parents in French. Then the father answered in heavily accented English. "Two nights."

"Did you meet Father O'Malley?"

"*Oui*. We went to Mass the day before he ..." the father searched for a word, then made a gesture with his hands as if Father O'Malley had gone up in smoke, "poof."

"How about you?" Danny turned to Nigel and his wife.

Both spoke at once. "We haven't been here long." Eleanor fell silent and her husband continued. "Couple days. We'll be leaving shortly."

"Do people from Birmingham often go to Ireland on vacation?"

"Nigel's doctor suggested a restful holiday," Eleanor explained. "His back has been giving him trouble."

"What sort of work are you in, Mr. Greene?" Danny asked.

"I'm a contractor," he said, fumbling with a medication bottle. His joking manner vanished. He took two pills from the bottle and washed them down with tea.

"Builds flats for the government," his wife added.

Danny rose from the table. "I've had a long, upsetting day," he apologized. "Will you excuse me?"

"But you haven't finished your tea, sure," said Mrs. Slattery.

Danny smiled weakly. "I guess I don't have much of an appetite tonight."

As he climbed the stairs, he could hear the murmur of conversation resume below. He opened the door to his room and sat on the edge of the bed beneath the crucifix affixed to the wall and the painting of St. Martin de Porres.

Danny looked out the window to the failing light outside. Across the way he could see the green fields roll away toward the horizon and in the distance Desmond Conlon walking toward the village. The effect was melancholy, reminding Danny of a mournful Irish ballad—a lonely but beautiful sadness. With Father O'Malley gone, the emptiness of the green fields, once a welcome sight, now seemed oppressive.

For a full minute Danny struggled to keep his emotions under control. Finally he let his head drop into his hands and gave in to sobs that lasted until he fell asleep, with the murdered Christ hanging over him on the crucifix above the bed.

Five

Later that evening Danny woke to the wind howling and rain beating against the window. Unable to get back to sleep, he put on a hat and raincoat and dashed across the street to Larkin's Pub. As he crossed over, a blue car screeched around the corner, almost hitting him. "Hey, watch out!" Danny yelled as the car pulled up to the entrance of Shannonside and a man in his late fifties stepped out of the passenger side.

Danny lingered in the doorway of Larkin's and watched the man holding an umbrella over his head as he talked to the driver of the car through the window. The man looked up and down the street, then walked quickly toward Shannonside and went in. The car disappeared.

There were four people inside the pub: Liam Flynn, Tim Mahoney, Brendan Grady, and Seamus Larkin. When Danny entered, Seamus came from behind the bar wiping his hands on a towel, and Tim and Brendan looked up from their stouts. Old Liam Flynn sat dozing in the armchair in front of the turf fire.

Since Danny had first met his friends from the

pub two years ago, Brendan, the youngest, had changed the most of the four men. He sported a mohawk haircut—dyed purple—and a ring in his left ear. He divided his time between Ballycara and Galway—though what he did in Galway was a mystery.

Tim Mahoney said to Danny, "We heard you and Fidelma found Father O'Malley."

Danny nodded. "I still can't believe it."

Liam Flynn hobbled up to Danny and extended his bony hand. Liam looked older, Danny thought, as if he had aged in three weeks. He always looked old, but now he seemed positively ancient. Danny grasped his weak hand and shook it.

"We're sorry you had to be the one to find him," said Liam, "God rest his soul."

"Me too," said Danny, his voice raspy.

Even Seamus Larkin, one of the most unfriendly men Danny had ever met, seemed concerned. He put his hand on Danny's shoulder. "Steady yourself, Dan." His big hand guided Danny to the bar. "Have a seat lad. You're looking in need of a pint."

"Thanks, Seamus."

"We all have to meet our maker one of these days. He's with God now," Seamus said, returning to his place behind the bar and setting up pints of stout.

The year before, Seamus had installed a big-screen telly in the pub. But only Liam Flynn paid any attention to the tractor pull being broadcast by SKY TV via satellite. The tractor pull took place in Austria and featured monster trucks driven by overweight Germans in baseball caps slopping around in the mud with a Strauss opera as soundtrack.

Seamus Larkin pulled a pint of Harp and brought it out.

"Here you are, Danny. Harp still your poison?" A trail of foam dripped down the side of the jar onto Seamus' hand.

"Thanks," said Danny, reaching for the pint.

Brendan Grady sipped his stout and ran his hand along the bristles of his purple mohawk. Liam Flynn pushed his glass forward for a refill.

The publican thrust a full pint into the old man's hand. "That'll be two pounds."

Danny pulled out a ten pound note. What the hell, he thought, in a rare moment of magnanimity, "This round's on me, Seamus." He twirled his finger. "All of them, on me."

The publican smiled. "It's about time you cleaned some of the cobwebs from your wallet."

Danny chuckled good-naturedly.

"Well," Tim Mahoney said, raising his own glass. "Here's to Father O'Malley. God rest his soul."

"Sure, we're going to miss him," Flynn said. "What in God's name do you suppose happened? A stroke?"

"I don't know," Danny responded. He pulled up a chair in front of the fire beside the old man and studied Liam's face. The scene of death flashed through Danny's mind and he shuddered. "It was the oddest thing, the way he was laid out."

Liam Flynn thumped his chest. "Probably the ticker."

"Maybe," said Danny. "You were at Mass this morning, weren't you, Liam?"

"I was."

"How did he seem?"

Liam considered the question. "Sure, wasn't I concentrating on me prayers, and not on the pastor's state of health?"

"Did you see him after Mass?" Danny followed up.

"I did not. Normally he'd come out of the sacristy after Mass and go around to the front of the church and talk to the congregation as they left."

"But he didn't do that?" Danny sipped his Harp, letting it burn his tongue.

"He did not. Now that I think of it," Liam mused, "'twas a bit queer."

"Did everyone at Mass leave the church soon after?"

"We all came out together, more or less, I'd say."

"What about altar boys?"

"Just one," Liam answered. "Little Jeremy Malloy."

Danny made a mental note of the name. He paused. "Who else was at church, do you know?"

"I do. There were nine of us: Me; Mrs. Slattery; Kathleen Conlon and her son, Desmond; Nigel Greene; Peggy Malloy—"

"That's the woman who moved down here from Dublin last year, isn't it?"

"That's right. Her son Jeremy was serving Mass."

"You've mentioned seven people. You said there were nine at Mass."

"If you'd let me finish." Liam ticked off the fingers on his right hand again, reciting the names. "Mrs. Slattery; Widow Conlon; Desmond Conlon; Nigel Greene; Peggy Malloy; Jeremy Malloy; me; Seamus; and James Roche."

"Who is this James Roche?" Danny asked. He wondered if that was Roche who had gotten out of the car that almost hit him.

"Well, he's a bit of a queer one, sure. He just came here three weeks ago."

"Does he work?"

"No, he's redundant."

"What?" Danny asked, laughing.

"Redundant. Unemployed."

"Oh. How does he live?"

"I've heard he got a big sum of money in Australia."

"I see. Where's he from?"

"Well, he's Irish, but he's been living in Australia for some time. They say he won the Irish Sweepstakes there and used the money to come home."

"How nice for him." Danny leaned back against his chair, set his pint of Harp down, and looked at Liam. "What about the curse on the rectory? Do you believe in that?"

"Believe in it?" Liam snorted. "I was the first to warn the damn fools not to build the rectory between those two ring forts. Sure, isn't it in a direct line between them."

"You don't really believe those old *pisoigs*, do you, Liam?" Seamus Larkin asked.

The old man took a long gulp of his stout and wiped the cream from his lips with the back of his hand. "You know what the old woman from Kerry said when Lady Gregory asked did she believe in fairies?"

"What's that?"

"She said I may not believe in 'em. But that doesn't mean they don't exist."

"What about you, Tim," Danny asked, turning to Tim Mahoney, who was talking quietly with Brendan. "What do you think about the curse of the ring forts? In fact, you're the first one who told me about it."

Tim took a deep breath as if preparing to pontificate. He dug in his right ear with his little finger and looked at the fingernail when he withdrew it. "Well," he said, "there have been a lot of unexplained cases of misfortune when people disturbed the stones around ring forts. Though I know none personally in which merely building in a direct line between two forts ever caused a problem. Until now," he concluded hastily.

"So," Danny prompted, "what do you really think?"

"Well, I'm not sure," said Tim. "Tomorrow is St. John's Day, you know, Midsummer in the old pagan calendar, and Father O'Malley was concerned with occult activities in Ireland."

"Did he have reason to be?" Danny asked.

"Perhaps. The gardai in Tullamore recently investigated satanic activity in a graveyard there." Tim took a sip of his stout. "There's also said to be some strange groups in and around Limerick, as well."

"Bunch o' cod," Seamus said from behind the bar, washing jars with his heavily veined hands. "I talked to Kelley on the phone just after you found him. He thinks Father O'Malley had a heart attack."

"But the door of the basement was locked behind him," Danny said. He did not mention that the priest's keys were missing.

"That means nothing," said Larkin.

"Well what," Danny asked in exasperation, "do *you* think happened to Father O'Malley?"

Brendan Grady slammed his jar of stout down on the bar and whirled around, his face mottled, forehead thickly creased. "I'm thinking it's extremists from the North."

Danny perked up. "What do you mean?" he asked.

"UDA fellows, or one of their lot," Brendan snapped.

"What's UDA?" Danny asked.

"Ulster Defense Association, the largest Protestant paramilitary group in Northern Ireland. They've loads of right-wing groups carrying out all sorts of mischief in the North. The UDA, the Ulster Volunteer Force, the Ulster Freedom Fighters. In America you never hear about them. All you ever hear about is what the IRA does. But the Loyalists have their own terrorist groups as well, you know. I'm surprised you haven't heard about them in Dublin."

"What does that have to do with Father O'Malley?" Tim Mahoney asked. "The poor man had a heart attack."

"I wouldn't put it past them to kill a Catholic priest in the Republic," said Brendan, his mohawk bobbing a bit as he shifted in his chair. "Wasn't there just a priest killed up in Monaghan not long ago by Protestant extremists?"

"Oh, Brendan," Liam Flynn said, "there you go again putting all of our troubles on the Protestants. Do you think that if all the Protestants in the world disappeared the Irish would be at peace with themselves?"

"Of course not," the bartender answered. "Sure,

wouldn't we find someone else to blame our own sorry state on."

Danny sipped his drink and pondered Brendan's theory. "Well, what about these extremists? What do you think they might have done?"

Brendan looked pleased with himself for having turned the discussion to politics. He took the floor as if he intended to hold it. "They probably murdered him," Brendan said.

Seamus Larkin groaned from behind the bar where he wiped jars with a rag. "Oh, for Christ's sake, Brendan. You're letting your imagination run away with itself."

"No," Brendan shot back, "they may have killed him in retaliation for one of their own lads, like the Provos do sometimes."

"Provos?" Danny asked. He had yet to master the complex vocabulary of the Northern Ireland conflict.

"The Provisional wing of the Irish Republican Army. The IRA split in 1969," Brendan lectured. "The Official wing stresses community-level activism to bring about better housing, education, and employment for the Catholic minority. The Provisional wing insists on a military solution to drive out the British and unite the thirty-two counties of Ireland." Brendan took a sip of his stout. "Or at least they *did* believe in a military solution. Now they're sitting down at the table with the Brits, and right there in Ennis, no less."

"Sure, you'd know more about the operations of the IRA," said Tim Mahoney, "than any of the rest of us, Brendan."

Brendan Grady took that as a compliment. "That's right. I would, wouldn't I?"

"Besides," Tim went on, "it's just as likely to be a splinter group—like the Irish National Liberation Army—trying to disrupt the talks in Ennis."

"What talks?" Danny asked.

"Where have you been, man?" said Brendan. "Prime Minister Tony Blair and Gerry Adams, Leader of Sinn Fein, are meeting for a round of talks at the Old Ground Hotel in Ennis next week."

"Oh, you're all jumping ahead of yourselves," Seamus Larkin pulled the discussion up short. "I'm sure Father O'Malley ..." Seamus seemed to falter a moment, "had a heart attack," he concluded haltingly.

"Father O'Malley was the picture of health," Liam Flynn put in.

"Well, you and I both know, Liam, that as devout as the good Father may have been, he still liked a drop of the Jameson as much as the next man."

Other than old Mrs. Finnarty, whom he had talked to on the bus, Danny had not heard anyone else in Ballycara venture this opinion of Father O'Malley. But the statement met with vocal protest from both Liam Flynn and Tim Mahoney.

"Are you slandering our P.P.?" Liam said angrily, standing up and knocking his chair over in the process. He snorted, fists up as if daring someone to box him.

Danny mentally translated the abbreviation: Parish Priest.

"Well, I'd not say," Seamus answered defensively, "that saying a man liked a bit of the drink is slander a-tall. Especially when it's said by a publican. If it weren't for people liking the drink I'd not have a job."

"Sure, Father O'Malley was great *craic* with a few jars in," said Tim Mahoney.

"That's right," said Liam.

"Now wait a minute," the publican began, then took a deep breath. "I'm just saying that maybe he just had a bit too much of the drink taken."

"You're talking about a saint of a man," Tim shouted. "And he died after nine-thirty Mass. What in heaven's name does that have to do with too much of the drink taken?"

"Well," Seamus said, "he might not have been the saint you make him out to be."

"What's that supposed to mean?" asked Flynn. "I'm thinking you're still mad, Seamus, that the priest wouldn't marry you and the Widow Conlon."

The conversation, like the last time Danny was here, had turned from reasoned discourse to chaotic shouting in less than ten minutes. Ah, the Irish, Danny reflected, sipping his pint. "What about the people staying at Shannonside?" he interjected.

"Who?"

"The English couple?"

"He's an ass," said Brendan Grady. "Came in here a couple nights ago with his silly jokes and capers."

Seamus Larkin, always quick to prove what a worldly man he was said, "You don't understand the English, Brendan. I lived fifteen years in England before I came back and bought this pub." With one hand on the pump, he continued. "I understand the English, and I thought he was a jolly fellow."

"Jolly fellow, me arse," said Brendan. "Sure, he wouldn't even have a jar with us."

Seamus pulled a fresh round of stouts behind the bar. "He's taking medication," he explained, "for his sore back."

"Then what's he coming into the pub for if he won't have a jar?"

"And the French couple?" Danny asked.

"Fine Catholic people," said Liam.

"How do you know?"

"They were at daily Mass the day before the priest disappeared."

"Liam," Danny said. "How well did you know Father O'Malley?"

"Sure, I knew him as well as the next man, I suppose."

"Was there anything unusual about the priest that I wouldn't know about?"

"Unusual?"

"Yes. Anything?" Danny still wondered what Father O'Malley wanted to confide in him.

"Not that I can think of."

"Did anyone have any grudges against him?" Danny asked.

Flynn glanced at the publican. "Of course not. You should know that, sure, you knew him as well as the rest of us."

"Of the eight people who were at his last Mass, which one do you think liked Father O'Malley the least?" Danny asked.

Liam Flynn seemed shocked by the question. "Sure,

I wouldn't know that any of us liked him less than any other."

"Did he have any enemies?"

"I wouldn't know," said Liam. He turned his back on Danny, packed his pipe with tobacco, and lit it with an ember from the fire. "The poor man had a heart attack," Liam mumbled around his pipe. "May he rest in peace."

Danny picked up his Harp and moved closer to the fire. "I thought I knew Father O'Malley pretty well," he said to Liam.

"I'm sure you did. Maybe better than the rest of us."

"But was there anything at all that Father O'Malley might have been keeping secret?"

"I'm sure he had no secrets."

"He was a wonderful man," said Tim.

Silence fell and they listened to the turf hiss in the grate.

"Well now," said Liam with a little cough, "there *was* a story."

"A story?"

Almost imperceptibly, the others drifted closer to Liam. Seamus came over and threw a couple more bricks of turf on the fire.

Liam smiled, guarding his story like a spoiled child guards the baseball cards he does not intend to give up easily. He picked up his pint, took a sip, smacked his lips, and set the jar down carefully. "It was said that when Father O'Malley was a young fellow, before he went off to the seminary, he was in love with a girl down in Glenmore."

"Not so unusual, I would imagine," said Danny.

"Well, no. Not of itself. But as the story goes, the girl and the young O'Malley were engaged to be married." Liam Flynn slurped from his Guinness again, and held his hands out to the fire to take the chill off them. "It's said that the girl's father was to give a piece of land to the couple. As the wedding day approached, Padraic O'Malley got cold feet." Flynn stretched his booted feet toward the fire. "And the next thing you know O'Malley up and joined the seminary."

"Really."

"'Twas a bit of a scandal down in Kerry, they say."

"Who was the girl?"

"That I've never known," said Flynn.

Danny sat in silence, mulling it over. Father O'Malley had certainly never shared this part of his life with Danny. But it threw no light whatsoever on his death.

"Who was closest to Father O'Malley in Ballycara?" Danny asked.

"What do you mean?" asked Flynn, sucking on his pipe.

"You know. His best friend."

Danny looked at the men. Seamus Larkin came around from the bar and the men in the pub watched him as he wiped his hands on a towel. "You know," he said, putting a hand on Danny's shoulder. "You might not realize it, but *you* were the best friend Father O'Malley had in Ballycara."

Danny looked up, surprised. "Me?"

"It's different with you, Danny," Seamus explained.

"You see, you're an outsider. The rest of us, well ..." His voice trailed off.

"He looked forward to your visits," Tim Mahoney finished for him. "I'm sure you two talked about things that he would have never talked about with us."

Danny's eyes had begun to water.

"He was mighty fond of you," said Seamus.

Danny took a sip of his Harp and struggled to control his emotions. He couldn't let himself break down in front of all these men. "Excuse me," he said, getting up. "I've got to use the bathroom."

In the bathroom, Danny splashed cold water on his face, combed his hair, took several deep breaths, then went back into the pub.

"Well," Danny said when he returned to his barstool, "I suppose it's best to leave it to the Garda Siochana now."

"You think Father O'Malley had a heart attack?" asked Seamus.

"There's something funny about this whole business," Danny answered.

"We've been talking," Brendan Grady began. "Here in the pub. Some of us think maybe Father O'Malley didn't die of a heart attack, either. You know, Kelley would have never found the killer of your cousin, Rose, two years ago if it hadn't been for you."

"Oh, I don't know about that."

"Anyway," Brendan glanced at his watch, "Kelley's somewhere in Spain by now."

Danny's temper flared. "I still can't believe he went on vacation at a time like this."

"He had no reason to believe it was anything but a heart attack."

"We were thinking," Brendan continued, "that maybe you could stay around—"

"Oh, no," Danny said hastily. "I can't. I have to get back to Dublin."

"You could postpone it," said Liam.

"I'm sorry," Danny said, picking up his pint and pulling his chair closer to the fire, as if even the thought of staying longer made him uncomfortable.

Seamus Larkin looked at Danny. "We're asking you, Danny. If you refuse, we'll not hold it against you. But could you stay here in Ballycara and see if you could find out something? If he didn't die of a heart attack, someone needs to find out what did happen. Father O'Malley thought the world of you, Danny. Don't do it for us, but for the love of God, do it for him."

Danny swallowed the lump in his throat and stood. Again he struggled to keep control. "I'm sorry," he managed to say. "I really am."

Danny finished his pint, stood up, and walked to the door of the pub. For a moment he thought of Father O'Malley. Never again would he hear his thick Kerry brogue or his cry of delight when a salmon had taken his fly on the River Shannon. Never again would he hear him murmur, "That's a good one," when he'd driven his golf ball far up the fairway. Never again would they share a quiet moment in the rectory over a glass of Jameson.

Danny opened the door and looked outside. Despite the rain, in the hills above the village, Danny saw the flames of half a dozen bonfires leaping and snapping like demons as the good Catholic people of Ballycara carried on the Midsummer traditions of their pagan ancestors.

When Danny turned back to the men in the pub to say goodbye they all looked at him expectantly. To his surprise he heard his own voice. "To begin with, there needs to be a postmortem. That would determine once and for all how Father O'Malley died. If an autopsy proves he died of a heart attack, then there'll be no need for me to stick around."

"That's right," said Brendan.

The men waited.

Outside, the blaze of the bonfires illuminated the night. "Okay," Danny said. "I'll see what I can do."

Six

Danny woke to a wet, windy morning. A swirl of soggy leaves rolled up the main street and blew over the open fields while the rain beat down in torrents. Behind Larkin's Pub, in a field of freshly-mown hay, a flock of sheep with bright splotches of pink spray paint on their backs cowered against a tree. From his window, Danny watched Desmond Conlon, in a rain hat and slicker, stacking limbs that had blown down the night before beside Mrs. Slattery's garden. Danny looked at the clock on the table beside his bed: 9:30.

"Danny," Mrs. Slattery called from downstairs.

Danny started at the sound of her voice. "Yes?"

"I've a bit of breakfast ready for you."

Downstairs, Mrs. Slattery had set out brown bread, butter, scones, toasted white bread, cranberry preserves, and a pot of fresh tea. She had the telly tuned to a weather report. "A slack northeast airflow covers the eastern half of the country while gale force winds developing in the North Atlantic are expected to batter the west coast of Ireland by tomorrow morning."

"That's quite a storm blowing outside," Danny said.

"According to the telly it'll be much worse by to-morrow."

Danny sat at the dining room table, buttered a piece of brown bread and eyed the pot of tea. He sighed and poured himself a cup. He still could not believe Father O'Malley was dead. He wondered what Father had wanted to talk to him about.

Mrs. Slattery came out with with eggs, rashers, sausage, black pudding, and fried tomatoes. She moved more slowly than yesterday, as if burdened by the death of the priest.

"Am I the only one having breakfast?" Danny asked.

"The rest have already eaten theirs," she said wearily. "The Gilberts are off to the Cliffs of Moher today for a bit of sightseeing."

"Pretty wet out for that. What about the Greenes?"

"Still here."

"Really? There's not much to do in Ballycara."

"Sure, you're here," said Mrs. Slattery.

"The boys in the pub asked me to stay and find out what I could about Father O'Malley's death. I don't believe he had a heart attack."

Mrs. Slattery touched his shoulder as she set the plate in front of him, then sat down. She stared intently into her teacup as if trying to divine by the leaves. She sighed. "Poor Father O'Malley." Still gazing into her cup, she shook her head. When she looked up, her eyes gleamed with moisture.

Danny reached across the table and patted her hand. He speared a sausage, put it in his mouth, chewed, and washed it down with tea. "What parish did Father O'Malley come from before he came to Ballycara?" he asked.

Mrs. Slattery scratched her head. "I believe it was up in Donegal as I remember. But truth to tell, I'm not quite sure."

Danny buttered a scone. "There was an altar boy at Father O'Malley's last Mass."

"Little Jeremy Malloy, sure."

"Where does he live?"

"What would you want with that lad?"

"He might be able to tell me something about the priest." Danny took a bite of his scone. "Where he went after Mass ... something."

"Well, the Malloys live just out on the edge of the village. There's a place in the road called the Cobbler's Rock. Now that's something you might want to take a look at yourself. Down at the fork of the road there's a rock on the right-hand side with a little indentation in it."

Mrs. Slattery sipped her tea and settled back in her chair. "Well, years and years ago, you see, there was a wee man—a cobbler, sure—who would sit on that rock and repair shoes. If you'd a shoe with a broken buckle, or any sort of leather goods for horses and such, well, you'd bring it down to the rock and this man—he wasn't a bit over four feet tall—would be sitting there on his rock mending things for everyone who passed along the road. And to this day there's an indentation in the rock where he sat."

Danny smiled. "How long ago was that?"

"Oh, sure, 'twas years passed. In my father's time.

Now the Malloys live in that little house there on the right just beyond the Cobbler's Rock."

"They haven't lived here that long, have they?"

"Not at all. You see they were moved down here from Dublin. It's part of a development scheme to get people out of the big cities and relocate them to areas of the West that are dying from the emigration."

"I see. How are they settling in?"

Mrs. Slattery raised an eyebrow and glanced over her cup of tea. "I'm thinking Peggy Malloy was used to a lot faster life up in Dublin."

"Faster?"

Suddenly, a violent banging startled both of them. Danny looked out the window and saw that the wind had blown an aluminum trash can against the front gate.

Mrs. Slattery leaned forward and her voice dropped to a whisper. "I've heard tell she was mixed up in the drugs up there."

"Really?"

"And don't think we haven't our own problems here in Ballycara with the young folks taking this Ecstasy and going to these Raves and all the rest of it into the bargain. I suppose you've seen Brendan Grady with his purple hair. Well, let me tell you, last week it was pink. The things he's picking up in Galway ... the Lord have mercy on us!"

Danny sipped his tea. "This James Roche ... what's he doing in Ballycara?" He wondered if it was Roche he had seen last night getting out of the car outside the pub. The car that nearly ran him over.

"No one knows for sure. He's a very private man."

"Does he have family in the area?"

"Not that I know of. It's been said he's from Kerry. I'm told he went to Australia, worked for twenty years. Played the Irish Sweepstakes every year. One year didn't he win enough to come back and retire in Ireland. I suppose he has no family left."

"Where's Mr. Roche now?" Danny asked. "Is he having breakfast with us?"

"Mr. Roche rarely eats with us, Danny. I suppose he prefers to eat by himself."

"Why?"

"Sure, I wouldn't know," she said, "nor is it my place to ask."

"He was at Father O'Malley's last Mass, wasn't he?"

"He's at Mass every morning," said Mrs. Slattery, and with that she disappeared into the kitchen and returned with more bread and a fresh pot of tea which she set in the middle of the table.

"You were at Mass yesterday. Was there anything odd—I mean did Father act strangely?"

Mrs. Slattery pondered the question for a moment. "Well, he did seem a bit sluggish, and yes, there was something odd."

"What?"

"He asked that when we say our Rosary at home and in the Novena this month we meditate on the Second Sorrowful Mystery—the Scourging of Christ by the Roman soldiers. For a special intention, he said."

Danny remembered that when he found the priest, Father O'Malley had been holding his rosary.

"And the sermon was a bit queer for Father O'Malley."

"How so?"

"Well, again he talked about the Second Sorrowful Mystery. And he read a passage from our Novena booklet."

"What was the passage?"

Mrs. Slattery heaved herself from her seat, shuffled across the room, and picked up a booklet from the coffee table: *Rosary Novenas To Our Lady* by Charles V. Lacey. She flipped through the book until she found what she was looking for. "Here. This is it, the section on the Sorrowful Mysteries." She handed the booklet to Danny.

Danny read the prayer before the recitation. "'At thy feet I humbly kneel to offer thee a Crown of Roses—blood-red roses to remind thee of the passion of thy divine Son, with Whom thou didst so fully partake of the bitterness—each rose recalling to thee a holy mystery.'"

Danny looked up at Mrs. Slattery who nodded and said, "Go on."

"The Scourging. 'O most sorrowful Mother Mary, meditating on the Mystery of the Scourging of Our Lord, when, at Pilate's command, thy divine Son, stripped of his garmets and bound to a pillar, was lacerated from head to foot with cruel scourges and His flesh torn away until His mortified body could bear no more. I bind these blood-red roses with a petition for the virtue of Mortification and humbly lay this bouquet at thy feet.'"

Danny closed the book. "Mortification?"

"Self-inflicted pain."

A horrible thought occurred to Danny: Could Father O'Malley have committed suicide?

A loud crash outside made Danny jump, and Mrs. Slattery stood up. "Good Lord, what was that?"

Danny looked out the window and saw that a huge branch had been broken by the wind and fallen into the front yard. "A branch got knocked down," Danny said. Then: "What was his sermon about?"

"What?"

"Father O'Malley's sermon."

"He spoke of the suffering we have in life." Mrs. Slattery looked down at her hands and then back to Danny. "He talked about repentance, atonement, and the sacrifices we have to make."

"What kind of sacrifices?"

"Sure, wouldn't that be different for each person. Now you take Seamus Larkin who has to take care of his dear mother who's sick with the diabetes. 'Tis been a burden on him. Father O'Malley would say that we've to be strong under these tests that the Lord gives us. He said even a priest might have a bitter pill to swallow in life."

"Sounds like a pretty regular sermon to me." Danny moved the Novena booklet aside and returned to his breakfast.

"Well, 'twas, in a manner of speaking. But there was something about the way he delivered it." Mrs. Slattery fidgeted with a carving knife that sat next to the loaf of bread in the center of the table. "Sure, I'm imagining things, I suppose."

"No. What?"

"It was as though *he* was asking forgiveness for something."

"Really?" Danny murmured.

"It was not like Father O'Malley to be so solemn. Ah, sure he'd go on his tirades about the usual things: divorce, abortion, and especially about paganism. But he never turned things to himself too often."

"Do you think Father O'Malley had a heart attack?"

"I really don't know."

A moment of silence passed, then Danny asked, "Why did Nigel Greene go to Mass yesterday? He isn't even Catholic. I noticed they didn't bless themselves after grace last night."

Mrs. Slattery sliced a piece of bread from the loaf and buttered it. "He said he wanted to 'experience' a Mass in Ireland."

"Did you see him after Mass?"

"Yes. We walked to church together, sat together, and walked back to Shannonside after Mass."

"You sat together?"

"Yes."

"Was he on the aisle?"

"He was."

"He never left your sight?"

"No." She looked at Danny, the knife still in her hand. "We were together the entire time."

"Where did he go when you got back to Shannonside?"

"To his room."

"His wife didn't go to church with him?"

"No."

Danny picked at his eggs with his fork. "Do you know anybody who might have had a grudge against Father O'Malley?"

"I've no idea, really. What are you thinking?"

"Well, I'm just not sure," Danny said. "He never argued with any of the parishioners?"

"Well, now, he and Dr. Cassidy never got along."

"Oh, really? Why not?"

"Sure, I shouldn't be spreading gossip," Mrs. Slattery began, but it was obvious she loved doing it. "Dr. Cassidy doesn't believe in our abortion laws in this country. You know it's illegal here. And, God forbid, the Church doesn't approve of it. But it's been said that more than one of our girls has gotten pregnant and Dr. Cassidy helped them get to England where they had abortions. Well, when Father O'Malley got wind of it, he threw Dr. Cassidy and his wife out of the church. Forbids them to enter the doors."

"Is that so? I always thought Father O'Malley was well liked in Ballycara."

"God rest his soul," Mrs. Slattery began, "but Father O'Malley was not the easiest man to get along with."

That surprised Danny. "How so? We had great times together."

Mrs. Slattery cut another piece of bread. "It was different with you. It's hard to explain, really," she said, looking away from the table for a moment. "He was a man of the earth, sure. Born and bred on a farm down in Kerry. So he should have understood his people here in Ballycara."

"I thought he did."

"Well, don't take offense, but it always seemed to me he was more interested in the golf club crowd in Kilkee and Lahinch than the ordinary people of his parish."

"It's not a sin to play golf."

"No, it's not." She pointed the knife at Danny. "But sometimes it seemed like he was just here to minister to the needs of his poor backward country cousins, although he prefered to spend his time with the sporting crowd up in Ennis."

For the first time, Danny's image of Father O'Malley as a kind, loving pastor began to crack. "Was that the kind of priest Father Longley was?" Danny asked. Michael Longley had been Father O'Malley's predecessor.

Mrs. Slattery glanced at Danny and held the knife aloft. "Not a-tall. Father Longley was one of the finest priests I ever met in my life. He cared for *all* of his flock, rich and poor alike."

Danny chewed his bacon silently and eyed Mrs. Slattery. "What do you think this bitter pill Father O'Malley mentioned in his sermon was?" he asked.

She cut another slice of bread and set it on Danny's plate. "Sure, I thought he was referring to a health problem."

"Was he suffering from something?"

"Not that I know of."

"Or maybe there was someone that he was afraid of. Someone who had threatened him."

Mrs. Slattery closed one eye and tilted her head to

look at Danny out of the other. "I'm thinking that would be stretching."

Danny shrugged. "I don't know. But then if he had a heart attack or something ... no, it doesn't make sense. I think he must have had something heavy weighing on him. I mean," Danny added, wondering if Mrs. Slattery would understand the slang, "heavy!"

"Aye."

Mrs. Slattery picked up the knife and as she sliced into the bread, the knife slipped and she cut deeply into her thumb. She yelped with pain, and dropped the knife, which clattered on the floor.

"Are you alright?" Danny asked, jumping up.

Blood pooled in Mrs. Slattery's palm like stigmata and dripped onto the table.

The doorbell rang.

Mrs. Slattery stood up as Fidelma Muldoon opened the door and ran in, her hair soaked and dishevelled from the rain and wind. "No need to get up," she said to Mrs. Slattery as she came over to the table and set a paper bag down. "I've brought a few things over from Carmody's shop."

Fidelma looked haggard, her eyes red-rimmed and swollen, as if she had wept all night. "My God, what's happened?" she gasped, pointing at the blood on the table.

"Just an accident," said Mrs. Slattery who had wrapped her hand in a dishcloth.

"Let me see."

"I'm fine."

"Are you sure?"

"It's nothing," said Mrs. Slattery, waving them away. She picked up the bag and carried it into the kitchen.

"Is she all right?" Fidelma asked. "Should I call Dr. Cassidy?"

"She'll be okay."

Fidelma took off her coat and laid it across a chair. "So, I understand the boys at the pub asked you to stay on for a few days."

Danny smiled awkwardly. "Yes. I think an autopsy needs to be done."

"I'm scared, Danny."

"Scared?"

"You know as well as I do that Father O'Malley didn't die of a heart attack. Something awful happened here. I spoke to the bishop on the phone this morning and he's no help a-tall. Sure, and he spoke as if Father O'Malley's been transferred to another parish. He doesn't seem at all concerned about finding out what happened to him. Leave it to the Garda Siochana, he says."

"What's the bishop's name?" Danny asked, standing up.

"Bishop Hamil." Fidelma rubbed at the worry line between her eyes. "Have you found anything?" she asked. "There must be something you can do."

Danny's temper flared like the flame on a Zippo. "I intend to call the bishop right now."

Fidelma reached into her purse and took out a card. "Here's the number."

Danny looked down at the card. "Don't worry. We'll figure this out."

"Do you have any ideas?"

"Well, I know this. Somebody locked the basement door after him."

"Who?"

"I don't know, but I intend to tell the bishop myself that there needs to be an autopsy."

Fidelma went to check on Mrs. Slattery while Danny dialed the office of the chancery. After explaining his reason for calling to half a dozen people, he finally got through to the Right Reverend Bishop Timothy Hamil of County Clare.

They discussed the funeral arrangements briefly, but when Danny broached the subject of an autopsy, the bishop was less than enthusiastic.

"We live in an age, young man," Bishop Hamil said paternally, "in which we are constantly seeking an explanation for God's divine plan. Or trying to assign blame when God's plan does not go the way we think it should."

"All I'm saying is that an autopsy would put to rest any doubts about the way Father O'Malley died."

"I spoke to Chief Superintendent Burke yesterday evening," said the Bishop. "He seems to have no doubts at all."

"But I do, and quite a few of his parishioners seem to doubt that he had a heart attack, or whatever they're calling it."

"Young man, the body is a sacred vessel of the soul. Even in death, it should not be desecrated."

"But an autopsy—"

"I understand how upset you are," the bishop said.

"But life and death are in God's hands. None of us knows the hour or the day we'll be called, and when Father O'Malley made an appointment to see me this week, only God knew he would never make it."

"He had an appointment to see you?"

"That's right. Wednesday at two o'clock."

"What about?"

"I'm not sure, really. He just said he wanted to talk."

"Was that unusual?"

The bishop said nothing.

"Your Eminence, please. I believe Father O'Malley may have been murdered."

"I will take your concerns," said the bishop before hanging up, "into consideration."

Seven

"Are you sure you want to see this?" the deputy state pathologist for County Clare, Anna O'Leary, asked.

Danny's call to the bishop and half a dozen calls to Chief Superintendent Burke had finally produced results.

"Yes," Danny said, "I'm sure." In reality he wasn't at all sure he was prepared to view the body of his friend, Father O'Malley, laid out on an autopsy table.

"This is highly unusual," Dr. O'Leary said as she led Danny down a flight of stairs at Ennis General Hospital. "But I understand you're the one who insisted that there be a post-mortem examination."

"That's right."

"Chief Superintendent Burke said you've been a real pain in the behind, but you're to have access to whatever information we have."

At the foot of the stairs, they entered what appeared to be an examining room. "I'm not sure I approve. But I'm holding Burke responsible for this."

Dr. O'Leary opened a box of disposable green surgical scrubs. "Put these on," she said to Danny, as she stepped into her own scrubs.

Danny put the plastic suit on over his clothes.

Dr. O'Leary handed him what appeared to be a box of tissue, and Danny pulled from it a pair of sterile plastic booties to fit over his shoes.

Finally, after putting on latex gloves, Dr. O'Leary opened a door and Danny followed her into a room of white tile and chrome. In one corner stood a metal cart used for transporting bodies to the morgue. In another stood a scale, like one you would see in a produce market. But this one was for weighing the organs that had been removed from the body.

Danny felt woozy, but he steadied himself. After all, he had asked to come here. Now that he was here, however, he regreted promising the guys in the pub that he'd look into Father's death. Then he saw the shiny aluminum autopsy table itself with holes drilled into the bed to allow water and fluids to drain, and he felt his knees go weak, and thought for sure he would faint.

"Are you all right?"

Danny nodded and looked around, but to his relief he did not see a body.

Dr. O'Leary moved to a small metal desk, opened a file folder lying on top, and removed a sheaf of papers. "This is the autopsy report," she said, handing the papers to Danny. "It outlines the results of my dissection and examination of the body."

He isn't a body, he wanted to say to her, his name is Padraic O'Malley.

Dr. O'Leary picked up a phone on the desk. "Will

you send in case number eight five six eight. Room number three."

Within a few minutes two attendants in green scrubs wheeled in a cart covered with a white sheet.

"I'm not sure," Danny whispered, "if I can go through with this."

Danny was no stranger to corpses. Having been raised above his father's funeral parlor in New York, he had been around dead bodies most of his life. But this was different.

"Sure, you're the one who requested this. I told you I don't approve of your being here a-tall."

Danny steadied himself. "Go ahead."

Dr. O'Leary flipped back the sheet, exposing the naked body of an elderly woman.

Danny gasped.

Dr. O'Leary had already picked up the phone. "I said case number eight five six eight, you half-wits!"

The attendants scurried back in with another cart and wheeled the old woman out.

"I don't know what's happening to this country," Dr. O'Leary scowled, and before Danny could respond she pulled back the sheet.

Father O'Malley lay on the cold metal table. To see a priest in street clothes without his vestments had always been a slight shock to Danny. To see Father O'Malley's body completely nude and laid out on an autopsy table nearly did him in.

"As you see here," Dr. O'Leary began in her professional monotone, pointing to the priest's stomach, "there is a scar in the right lower quadrant of the abdomen."

"Was he stabbed?"

"No. Prior surgical excision of the vermiform appendix."

"What?"

"An old scar, where his appendix was removed. An autopsy report must contain a complete description of the body."

"I see." Danny forced himself to look back at the dead priest.

"As you will note, the victim was in good physical shape for his age."

"You bet he was," Danny said. "He could beat me any day on the golf course, and we fished some pretty rough waters."

"Yes," Dr. O'Leary said disinterestedly. "Rigor mortis was not well established at the time of the body's discovery, which was—"

"About six o'clock," Danny said. "The sacristan of the church and I found him in the basement."

"Right. Now, as you can see, there are some lacerations here," Dr. O'Leary turned one of Father O'Malley's hands palm up, "on the wrists and hands."

Danny bent down for a closer look. "Looks like scratches."

"Defense wounds."

"What?"

"It seems likely that the victim struggled with someone immediately before his death."

Danny closed his eyes and tried to squelch the image of Father O'Malley fighting for his life.

"Mr. O'Flaherty," the doctor said, annoyed, "we don't have to go on with this."

"No. Please, continue."

She pointed to a long scratch down the priest's hairy forearm. "These scratches were likely sustained while the victim defended himself against his attacker. Now, if you'll look here on the left anterior chest wall. Do you see this tiny red mark?"

Danny bent down and looked to where Dr. O'Leary pointed above Father O'Malley's left nipple. "Just barely."

Dr. O'Leary removed a magnifying glass from an overhead cabinet. "Here." She handed it to Danny.

He took the glass and looked at the red mark, then glanced at Dr. O'Leary. "It's like a pinhole."

"Apparently, a syringe was inserted into the victim's chest, near the heart. I've just now gotten the results of the blood tests."

"What did you find?" Danny asked, his voice trembling.

"First, a slight trace of alcohol in the bloodstream."

"Of course," he said defensively. "He'd just said Mass. He'd taken wine at Communion."

"Yes. Also, there were traces of poison in the bloodstream."

"Poison?"

"It appears that someone injected the priest with a mixture of several toxic compounds."

"No! How in the world could anyone have held him down long enough to inject something into him?"

"It seems likely he was sedated before he was injected with the poison."

"You mean someone drugged him, pushed him down in the basement, then injected him with poison?"

"Yes, something like that."

"Wouldn't the sedative show up in the blood as well?"

"Of course. There was quite a dose of Pethidine in the bloodstream in addition to the poison."

"Pethi-what?"

"Pethidine. It's a painkiller. Meperidine Hydrochloride. We found a substantial quantity of it in the victim's blood."

"How horrible," Danny mumbled.

"The sedative and the poisons were all that was found in the bloodstream. But it was more than enough to kill him. Death would have been fairly rapid."

"Have you determined a time of death?"

"Roughly ten-fifty a.m., June twentieth."

"Dr. O'Leary," Danny said quietly. "As a pathologist, what is your professional assessment as to the manner of death?"

"An autopsy can only offer an *opinion* on the manner of death."

"I'm asking for your opinion."

"Available evidence, particularly the lacerations on the hands and arms, strongly suggests that the victim struggled with someone immediately prior to death, and was subsequently injected with a mixture of highly toxic substances."

Danny, already struggling to keep his emotions in check, finally cried out in frustration, "Say it!"

Dr. O'Leary looked at him. "It is my opinion that Father O'Malley was murdered."

***

Danny found Chief Superintendent Burke outside the Old Ground Hotel in Ennis, directing a group of officers who were setting up security for the peace talks scheduled to open on Monday. Danny had the autopsy report in hand.

"Mr. O'Flaherty," the garda said, shaking hands with Danny when he had introduced himself. "I guess I owe you an apology. Dr. O'Leary called me earlier."

"No apology necessary."

"It looks like you were right."

Burke was a distinguished-looking, silver-haired gentleman, well-groomed and fit in his dark blue garda uniform. "If I had known this thing would turn out this way, I would have asked Kelley to postpone his holiday."

"There's no way you could have known."

A radio crackled on Burke's hip. He took it off his belt and spoke to an officer on the roof of the hotel, then directed two other officers to join the man on the roof.

"We're just monumentally busy," he apologized, "with these talks coming up."

"I understand."

"This thing is a security nightmare. I don't know why they didn't host the talks in Dublin."

"About Father O'Malley—" Danny began.

Another burst of static signaled a second call on Burke's walkie-talkie, and Danny followed him around to the back of the hotel where another group of officers set up barricades. When he finished talking to the other gardai, Burke turned to Danny.

"Since Kelley's out of the country," Danny asked, "will you be sending someone to Ballycara to investigate the murder?"

Burke gave Danny a pained look. "As you can see, we're short-handed. Every garda in the country is going to be here to help with security. I won't be able to spare a man to send out to Ballycara for at least a week."

"A week?"

"Impossible any sooner," Burke said, but was interrupted by a garda with a question about parking. As the Chief Superintendent talked to the other garda, Danny saw someone who looked familiar get out of a blue Peugot in the parking lot. When Burke had dealt with the interruption he continued. "You know, you did a bang-up job finding the murderer of your cousin two years ago. I thought maybe you could help us out on this one. I have Kelley's report and the photographs of the crime scene in the car. If you could interview witnesses and find out everything you can, we could get a jump on this thing by the time Kelley gets back. By then I'll also have a few other men to spare, once these talks are finished."

"I'd need help ..." Danny began.

"Of course. Our forensics team and crime lab here in Ennis can handle anything you send over to us. We just need a man on the job out there. I know this is a little unusual, but your instincts have been on target from the beginning. I have complete confidence in you."

"Well," Danny was a bit taken back, "I appreciate that."

"So, you'll lend a hand?"

Danny smiled. "Like I told the boys in the pub, I'll see what I can do."

"Brilliant."

The radio on his hip squawked again and Chief Superintendent Burke took off at a trot as he shouted into the walkie-talkie. "Call me tonight," he yelled over his shoulder to Danny.

As Danny made his way across the parking lot, it dawned on him that the familiar figure he saw getting out of a car moments before was James Roche.

What in the world was he doing here?

Eight

By the time Danny got back to Ballycara, the expected storm bent trees over and whipped the houses and fields with lashes of rain.

It was not the only storm to hit Ballycara. RTE, the national television network, had set up a van beside the church to broadcast a live report on the murder of Father O'Malley.

Danny, in raincoat and rubber boots, was ambushed by a crowd of reporters as he tried to get through the front door of Shannonside. "I understand you're the one who found the priest's body."

"Do you think the murder is connected to the talks in Ennis?"

"We understand you've been deputized by the gardai. Do you have any suspects yet?"

Danny waved the reporters away, dropped the autopsy report, Kelley's report, and the photographs of the crime scene in his room, exited the B&B through the back door, and sprinted to the edge of the village. Just past the Cobbler's Rock he waved to Desmond Conlon, who crouched beneath a tarp fixing a flat tire on a tractor in McMahon's pasture.

At the far end of the pasture, a small turquoise house squatted nearly hidden behind a stand of bending sycamores and overgrown hedges. A chimney rose from each end of the house. The yucca plant by the front door looked like something seen in California or Spain rather than Ireland. As Danny approached, an Irish setter, barking furiously, raced from behind the house.

Someone called the dog from inside. A woman who looked as if she had just gotten out of bed peered around the door. She had a hole pierced in the right side of her nose where she wore a silver ring. Her straw-colored hair was cropped short, and she had the starved look of a refugee. "What do you want?" she asked.

"My name is Danny O'Flaherty," he said, stepping up the front steps out of the rain. "I was wondering if I could speak with Jeremy?"

The woman blocked the door as Danny approached. "Are you from the school?"

"No," Danny answered.

"The press?"

"No, I'm from Dublin."

"And what would you want with my Jeremy? Is he in some kind of trouble?"

"Not at all."

"Did you find our cat?"

"Pardon me?"

"The boy's cat is missing. He wandered out in the storm and hasn't come home yet. I thought perhaps you found it."

"No," Danny answered. "I'm looking into the death

of Father O'Malley. We found him dead in the basement of the church."

"I know," Peggy Malloy said.

"An autopsy was done at Ennis General Hospital," Danny continued. "Father O'Malley was murdered."

"Murdered?"

"That's right, and Jeremy served Mass that day. I thought I might ask him some questions. And you too, if you don't mind. You were at Mass the morning the priest died, weren't you?"

"Who are you to be asking questions?"

"The gardai in Ennis asked me to look into this while Kelley is away."

The woman seemed to go limp from exhaustion, turned and called into the house, "Jeremy!"

To Danny's surprise, the little redheaded fellow he had met on the bus the day before came out and stood by his mother, who still blocked the door. He held a book in one hand and blinked at Danny through his oversized glasses.

"I remember you," the boy said, his eyes widening.

"He's looking into Father O'Malley's death," his mother told the boy.

"Are you a detective?"

"Well," Danny said, scraping his shoe on the step. "Not exactly. May I have a word with you?" he asked the boy's mother.

Peggy Malloy put her hands on her son's shoulder and moved him away from the door as if he were a chessman. "Make it quick," she said. "I've to put supper on the table."

Danny stepped inside the house which smelled of boiled cabbage, old laundry, and dog. The Cranberries played on a boom box on the floor. Mrs. Malloy led them into the sparsely furnished living room and Danny took a seat on the couch. On the coffee table in front of the couch lay a pack of tarot cards and an assortment of crystals. On the telly, a news anchor jabbered about the impending peace talks.

"Is your husband home?" Danny asked.

The woman exploded into bitter laughter. "That's a good one," she said without elaborating. She picked up a package of Drum tobacco and rolled a cigarette.

At least she didn't offer me tea, Danny thought, relieved. "Mrs. Malloy," he began, "I understand you had a key to the basement of the church."

Peggy Malloy looked up, startled, then put a match to the tip of her cigarette with shaky hands. She drew in a deep breath, tipped her face toward the ceiling and released a cloud of smoke. "I did."

"Do you still have it?"

"I don't."

Jeremy Malloy sat on the far side of the sofa with his book on his lap and stared at Danny with his mouth slightly open as if he were asthmatic. "Can you help me find my cat?" the boy asked.

"Sure. Be happy to. In the meantime, I understand you served Mass the morning Father O'Malley died," Danny said. "Did anything unusual happen that morning?"

The boy pondered the question a moment then said, "Father O'Malley seemed tired."

"Really? What made you think that?"

"He forgot some of the prayers. He never does that."

Jeremy Malloy had the manner of a person much older than he appeared and Danny wondered what kind of life the Malloys led. Peggy Malloy had finished her cigarette and drifted into the kitchen.

"When did you last see Father O'Malley?"

"Well," Jeremy began, adjusting his eyeglasses, "after Mass I went into the sacristy and changed out of my surplice. I was in a hurry. Father O'Malley was standing in front of the table where he takes off his vestments."

"Did he seem nervous or anything?"

"I don't know. He just seemed tired."

"Was there anyone else in the sacristy?"

"No," Jeremy said, then cocked his head as if remembering something.

"Are you sure?"

"Just me and Father."

"Both before and after Mass?"

"That's right."

"You're sure no one was in the sacristy before Mass?"

Jeremy lifted his shoulders in a shrug and let them drop. "No," he said, gazing down at his hands. "No one else came to the sacristy." The boy laced his hands together, turned them inside out and wiggled his fingers.

"Did Father O'Malley usually go to the entrance of the church after Mass and greet the congregation when they walked out?"

"Sometimes."

"Did he do that on the morning we're talking about?"

"I don't know. I went home as soon as I'd hung up my surplice."

Danny turned his attention to the telly when he heard the anchor, Ann Doyle, say: "Our Religious Correspondent, Joe Little, is live from Ballycara in County Clare."

A reporter stood in the doorway of St. Bridget's in a raincoat and hat shouting above the noise of the howling wind. "This normally sedate village on the westernmost tip of the Loop Head Peninsula has been ripped apart by the second murder in as many years. Results of an autopsy revealed that on Sunday of this week, the beloved parish priest, Father Padraic O'Malley, was drugged, dragged to the basement of this church where I am standing, and injected with a lethal cocktail of poisons."

"Any idea who might have done this?" the anchor asked.

"Sources close to the investigation ..."

"What sources?" Danny mumbled as Jeremy's mother came out of the kitchen and stood in front of the telly.

"...have speculated that the murder may be linked to talks between Prime Minister Tony Blair and representatives of Sinn Fein, including Gerry Adams, being held in nearby Ennis."

When the broadcast turned to sports, Danny turned to the boy's mother. "What about you, Mrs. Malloy?" Danny asked her. "Where did you go after Mass?"

"I came straight home," she said, putting her hand on the little boy's head and eyeing the clock on the wall.

Danny took that as a signal and stood. "May I use your ..." he could never get used to the Irish phraseology, "toilet?"

"It's in there," said Mrs. Malloy, pointing down the hall.

In the bathroom, Danny rummaged around looking for ... he wasn't sure what exactly. He saw the usual collection of items: shampoo, razors, Atrixo hand creme, mouth wash, Labello chap lipstick, toothpaste, calamine lotion, vitamin E skin oil. Danny opened the medicine chest. Inside he found a couple of prescription medications signed by Dr. Cassidy: Pamergan, Ciproflaxacin, an inhaler, Rynacrom nasal spray, a tube of ointment, vitamins.

Danny closed the chest, flushed the unused toilet, ran some water, and when a suitable interval had passed, went back into the living room.

"Well, you've been very helpful, Jeremy," he said to the boy.

"Are you going to find out who killed Father O'Malley?" Jeremy asked.

Danny looked at the boy. "I hope so."

"That's what detectives do, right? Look for murderers?"

"I'm not really a detective."

"Are you going to stake out the church?"

Danny laughed. "I don't think so."

"I bet that's what Columbo would do," Jeremy added.

"That's enough," said Peggy.

Danny hesitated a moment, then squatted in front of Jeremy and looked him in the eyes. "I want you to think, Jeremy. Just before Mass, did anyone talk to Father O'Malley?"

"You've upset him enough," Mrs. Malloy protested.

Jeremy watched Danny warily. His eyes shifted from his mother and back to Danny.

"Jeremy," Danny said gently. "You won't be in any trouble if you just tell the truth. Did anyone else come to the sacristy?"

The boy shook his head.

"Tell me this," continued Danny. "Did you bring the water and wine out before Mass or did Father O'Malley?"

"I always bring the cruets," the boy said, "and set them up on the little table in the aisle."

"Then at the consecration of the host you pour water over the priest's hands and he washes them. Then you pour the wine into the chalice and he drinks it."

"That's right."

"Did anyone mess with the cruets before Mass?"

Jeremy glanced quickly at his mother.

"Jeremy," Danny said, "you told me before that no one came into the sacristy. I won't be mad if you just tell me the truth now. It's important, son."

Jeremy looked at Danny and pushed his glasses up on his face. "Father O'Malley was going over his sermon," the boy said. "I was putting on my surplice. That's when the man came into the sacristy. I went to the sanctuary where I was after lighting the candles under the statue of the Blessed Virgin. As I was walking back in, I saw the man talking to Father O'Malley. By the time I got into the sacristy he was gone. It was just a glimpse of him I had."

"Who was it?"

"The old man. The one who lives at Shannonside."

"James Roche?"

"That's the one."

"What happened after that?"

"The old man left as I was going back into the sacristy. Father O'Malley said to take the water and wine into the church that we'd begin Mass right away."

Mrs. Malloy opened the door for Danny as if to indicate that they had answered enough questions.

"One more thing," he said to Jeremy. "When you left the sacristy after Mass did you see anyone outside?"

Again, the boy seemed deep in thought. "No."

"Are you sure?"

Jeremy pushed his glasses up on his face and scratched his head. He had the mannerisms of a little old man. "I did notice ... something."

"What?"

"Well, at the side of the graveyard, there was a car parked under the trees. Yeah. I remember that. I never saw that car in Ballycara before." The boy stared up at his mother as if seeking her approval. "And there was someone sitting in the car."

Danny's heart raced. "Really? Was it a man or a woman?"

"I couldn't see good enough. And I didn't remember it until just now."

"This could be very important, Jeremy. What kind of car was it?"

"I don't know."

Mrs. Malloy stepped between her son and Danny. "Isn't that enough, now? I don't want you upsetting the boy. His imagination is wild enough as it is without you planting a bunch of foolish ideas in his head."

"He's not planting ideas, Ma. There *was* a car there beside the graveyard. I saw it."

"Was it a big car? A little one?" Danny asked.

"I don't remember."

"I think that's enough now," the boy's mother said.

Danny grasped for one last piece of information. "What color was it?"

As Jeremy's mother moved the boy toward the kitchen he managed to say one more word. "Blue."

Danny stepped outside into the lashing rain and splashed back to the main road wondering about Jeremy's mother. Was she trying to hide something? She, too, was at Mass and seemed upset by Danny's visit. Maybe Father O'Malley had had a word with her about her past, or her tarot cards and New Age trinkets. The priest would undoubtedly have considered them pagan.

The wind tore at the trees and angry clouds rolled toward the village from the sea, bringing with them the smell of salt and kelp. An old Mercedes Benz plowed through the downpour with a bale of hay strapped to the luggage rack. The wind and rain plastered Danny's hair to his scalp.

Desmond Conlon had gotten the tractor started

and he drove toward Danny across McMahon's field. Danny, deep in thought about what Jeremy had told him, did not even look up as the tractor approached through the pouring rain.

When he realized that Desmond was driving straight toward him, Danny shouted and waved his hands, thinking Desmond was unable to see through the driving rain. But the tractor continued to bear down on him.

"Hey," Danny shouted as the tractor came out of the pasture and onto the road, headed straight for him. "Watch out!"

Danny moved to get out of the way, but was blocked by an earth embankment as the tractor turned and came at him again. "Stop!" Danny jumped aside but the huge back wheel of the tractor grazed his shoulder, knocking him down.

Danny lay on the road panting as Desmond, still oblivious to the accident, drove on toward home in the rain.

Nine

The funeral Mass for Father Padraic O'Malley took place in the cathedral in Ennis. Bishop Hamil of County Clare, and two priests who had been class-mates of Father O'Malley at Maynooth, concelebrated the Mass.

Danny had collected the chalice Father O'Malley used during his last Mass, the cruets, the bottle of altar wine, and the padlock to the basement, and sent them to Chief Superintendent Burke for examination in the crime lab in Ennis to check for fingerprints. Danny also asked that they check to see if any traces of the sedative could be found in the water or wine.

Danny and Fidelma drove the priest's Nissan Micra to Ennis for the Mass, but they did not go down to County Kerry where Father O'Malley was buried in his hometown of Glenmore. Rather, after the funeral they drove in silence toward Ballycara while the tail end of the storm sprayed raindrops on the windshield and blew debris across the road.

Fidelma had barely spoken on the drive to Ennis or throughout the Mass. They were halfway to Ballycara and she still stared silently out at the countryside of tumbledown cottages, modern ranch houses, and the hideous power transmission wires that marred the green Irish countryside.

Danny was telling Fidelma about his near miss with Desmond on the tractor, but she did not seem to be listening.

"Will you stay at the rectory and work for Father Murphy?" Danny asked, at last. The replacement for Father O'Malley had been announced that morning by the bishop.

Fidelma gazed out the window and shook her head. "I don't think so."

Danny expected as much.

"It's time for a change, Danny. I've been in Ballycara too long. There's a big world out there, and haven't I spent too many years looking after the sacristy and scrubbing the priest's dirty underwear?"

The bitterness in Fidelma's voice surprised Danny. "What will you do, then?"

"What do you mean, what will I do?" Fidelma asked. "Do you think all I'm good for is cleaning up after the clergy?"

"I didn't say that."

"But you were thinking it!"

"I was not."

"You were! And the way you and Kelley treated me the day we found Father O'Malley ... like I was good for nothing but to fetch things while you two great detectives muddled about with the corpse."

Fidelma's voice caught on the last word and she

buried her face in her hands. "I'm sick of this little village."

Danny didn't know what to say.

"And I'm leaving."

"Where?"

"Dublin to begin with. Then London or New York."

Danny was cheered by the thought that she would be in Dublin. "I could help you find a job," he offered.

But Fidelma said nothing.

Danny flicked on the wipers of the priest's car as the rain increased. It must have been stifling for her in Ballycara all these years. Indeed, it was time for a change, and he admired Fidelma for her willingness to make a move.

"When are you going?"

"Tomorrow morning."

"So soon?"

"There's nothing keeping me," she mumbled.

"Fidelma," Danny began. His doubts about Father O'Malley worried him more and more. "Be honest with me. What did you think of Father O'Malley?"

"He was wonderful."

"Be honest, Fidelma."

"I don't know what you're talking about. He was a wonderful man."

Danny began to wonder if his image of Father O'Malley as a devoted man of the cloth was realistic. "Mrs. Slattery told me he spent more time at the race-track in Listowel than with his parishioners."

"He had a right to a bit of the *craic*, didn't he? After all, you had plenty of good times with him."

"And golf in Lahinch?"

"He liked the good things in life," she said.

"Don't you have a right to some of the good things in life, too?"

Fidelma let out her breath. "I do," she whispered.

Danny fumbled with the radio and settled on a news broadcast. Startled by the urgency in the broadcaster's voice, he turned it up.

"No new developments in the murder of Father Padraic O'Malley of County Clare who was found dead in the basement of St. Bridget's Church in Ballycara earlier this week. Chief Superintendent Lawrence Burke of the Garda Siochana has dismissed speculation that the priest's murder may be linked to the peace talks being held in nearby Ennis."

Danny glanced at Fidelma, but she seemed in a state of shock as she stared out at the empty countryside.

"Did you hear that, Fidelma?"

Fidelma turned to him wearily. "I did."

"Do you think there might be a connection?"

"I don't know, Danny," she said, resting her head against the window. "I really don't know."

When they reached Ballycara, Danny asked Fidelma if he could go into the rectory and have a look around before Father O'Malley's things were removed to make room for the new priest.

"Will you have a cup of tea?" she asked when they were inside.

Danny grimaced. "Do you have coffee?"

"No. Sorry."

"Tea it is, then."

The first time Danny had been in the rectory two years ago, he and Fidelma had looked through the parish records for the baptismal dates of his grandparents. That seemed like ages ago. The rectory had been spruced up since then. The hardwood floors had been sanded and refinished and a new coat of cream-colored paint had been applied to the walls. All under the careful hand of Fidelma.

She led Danny through the foyer, and through the priest's study at the back of the rectory to the kitchen where she busied herself heating water.

"I haven't slept well," she said, "since the day we found Father O'Malley."

Danny sat down at the kitchen table. "When is his replacement getting here?" he asked.

"I'm expecting him tomorrow morning. I'll be leaving as soon as he arrives. He'll have to find a new housekeeper."

"I hope he can cook," Danny said wryly.

As Fidelma poured his tea, the steam fogged up Danny's glasses, so he took them off and laid them beside him on the table. "It must have been hard to find a replacement. I mean, with the curse on the rectory and all."

"Are you making fun of us?"

"No. But Father O'Malley is the fourth priest to die here."

Fidelma took her own tea and sat across from Danny. "Now, go ahead and see what you can find in Father O'Malley's study. You know I wouldn't let just anyone do that. I haven't looked around much myself. I've only boxed up a few of his things. I want you to see if you can find something that might give us a clue as to who did this."

Danny gulped his tea quickly and stood up. "I'll get started right now."

At one end of the priest's study stood a writing desk, bare except for a fountain pen in an ornate holder. Opposite, a set of bookcases held books on theology and religion, some on Irish history, and a few novels and books of poetry.

Father O'Malley loved reading, especially history. Many evenings he and Danny had sat together in this study discussing everything from the fall of the Roman Empire to the Easter Rebellion.

Danny opened the single drawer of the writing desk. The priest had never been a well-organized bookkeeper, Danny noted as he turned over invoices for work on the church, receipts from a laundry in Kilkee, scraps of hastily written shopping lists, cancelled checks written to Desmond Conlon, a three-year-old ticket stub from the Abbey Theatre in Dublin (*The Playboy of the Western World* by J.M. Synge), pencils, pens, Mass cards.

He sat in the priest's chair and rifled through the drawer without finding anything of interest. Frustrated, he pulled the drawer out of the desk completely and dumped its contents on top, setting the drawer aside on the floor. After combing the contents, he gave up and began replacing the items in the drawer when he noticed a yellowed photograph of Father O'Malley as a young man with his arm around a woman of the same age. Danny moved to the wing-back chair in front of the bookcase, turned the lamp on beside it, sat down, and studied the photograph. On the back was an inscription in the priest's hand. Father O'Malley wrote in the same florid script that Danny remembered from letters his grandparents had written. Strange, Danny thought, that even handwriting had its own unique Irish accent. "Glenmore," the inscription read, "1972." Danny remembered the story Liam had told about the girl from Glenmore.

"Find anything?"

Danny looked up, startled.

Fidelma Muldoon stood in the bedroom door.

"You scared me," he said.

"Sorry. Just wanted to know if you found anything of interest."

"Not really," Danny said, standing up. He put the photograph away, replaced the contents of the drawer, and put it back in the desk.

He continued his search of the room. When a thorough examination of the study failed to reveal anything of significance, he moved to the priest's bedroom. It contained a narrow bed with a crucifix over the headboard, a wooden wardrobe in a dark corner, and a window that overlooked the graveyard.

Danny opened the wardrobe and looked through the priest's clothes—mostly black pants and shirts. Two pairs of black leather shoes, a gray overcoat, one cassock.

"What was Father O'Malley wearing when he left the house for Mass on the morning he died?" Danny asked.

"He always changed into his vestments in the sacristy. He was wearing his usual outfit: black shoes, black socks, black pants, a short-sleeve black shirt and Roman collar, and black suspenders."

"The usual Catholic fashion statement," he laughed. "Did he seem worried about anything that morning?"

Fidelma cocked her head slightly as if to look at Danny from another angle. "Not as I can recall. Despite the harshness of some of his sermons, Father O'Malley, as you well know, was an easygoing man, sure."

"Was he in good health?"

"Dr. Cassidy warned him to watch his cholesterol." Fidelma hesitated. "That is, while Dr Cassidy was still his doctor. After he banned the doctor from church, Father O'Malley went to Kilkee for his medical care."

"Was he taking any kind of medication?"

"Not really. Vitamins."

"You said you were preparing his breakfast while he was at Mass. Did he ever eat before Mass?"

"Of course not. Just a cup of tea. He takes Communion at Mass, you know."

"Yes. He'd still be fasting. But he had a cup of tea before he left?"

"That's right."

Danny closed the wardrobe and moved about the room. "Do you think Father O'Malley was happy in Ballycara?"

Fidelma considered the question for a moment. "Sure, who's to say if he was happy. The life of a priest is not easy, you know. But if you want to know the truth, I don't think Father O'Malley was ever happier than when you used to come down from Dublin."

"We had some good times," Danny said. He paused. "Did anyone have any grudges against Father O'Malley that I wouldn't know about? Was there anyone in the parish that he argued with? I know he and Breda Slattery had their differences about the changes in the Church, and I heard about Dr. Cassidy, too. But can you think of anything else? Any disagreements of any kind?"

"Well ..." Fidelma began, then stopped. "Sure, I shouldn't be spreading gossip."

"If it's something that can help us find out who killed Father O'Malley, then I see no harm in it."

"The Widow Conlon and Seamus Larkin have approached the priest numerous times about getting married. They came to see Father O'Malley to ask would he marry them, and he'd hear nothing of it."

"Why wouldn't he?"

"I have no idea."

"He must have given some reason."

"He didn't discuss it with me. All I know is that the Widow Conlon has asked him every year since he's been the pastor and he has refused each time."

"You have no idea why?"

Fidelma studied the crucifix on the wall. "He had his reasons, I suppose."

"Why didn't they get married somewhere else?"

Fidelma gave a quick laugh. "This is not America, Danny. Ballycara is their home. If the parish priest of your own parish refuses to marry you, sure you don't go off looking for someone who will."

"When did she approach Father last on the subject?"

"Two days before he died she came to see him in the rectory after daily Mass."

"Did she come with Seamus?"

"Not this time. She was alone. I let her in and made tea while Father O'Malley changed out of his vestments. Don't misunderstand me. I was not eavesdropping. But when I brought the tea into his study I heard them talking. She was asking for the bans of marriage to be announced. Again Father O'Malley refused."

Danny puzzled over the problem. "Would you say," he asked, "that the replacement for Father O'Malley might look more sympathetically on her situation?"

Fidelma looked at Danny as if weighing the consequences of her answer before speaking. Finally, she said, "I don't know. Maybe. They say she has always been a bit miffed with Father O'Malley about it. That they'd had a kind of a tiff."

"What about Seamus? Was he angry about it?"

"I really don't know."

"Is she still seeing Seamus?"

Fidelma smiled. "You could say that."

"Do you think they'll ever marry?"

"I couldn't say."

Danny reached out and touched Fidelma's cheek. "What about you? When do you think you'll make some lucky guy the happiest man in the world?"

Fidelma's face turned a shade of crimson as bright as her hair.

"Well," Danny said, clearing his throat. He glanced at his watch. "There's nothing here. I guess I'd better be going. I'm going over to the pub." He needed the familiar atmosphere of the pub and a bit of conversation. "Care to join me? It's our last day together in Ballycara."

"I don't think so," Fidelma said, looking around. "I still have work to do."

Danny strode into the kitchen and took his jacket off the back of a chair. "I'd like to talk to Dr. Cassidy, too." He put his jacket on, took the tweed hat out of his pocket and snapped it on his head. "I'm off."

Fidelma walked him to the front of the rectory and opened the door to a bright, clear day. The storm had moved on, and he was amazed at how glorious the weather had turned. Danny let the sun warm his face, then turned and gave Fidelma a kiss on the cheek.

She whispered: "Find out who did it, Danny."

Ten

The next morning Danny met Fidelma in the open lot across from the Kilkee Business Centre where she had greeted him when he got off the school bus. Now they waited for the once-a-week Bus Eireaan to take Fidelma to Ennis where she would catch another bus to Dublin.

"Are you sure you want to do this?" Danny asked as she stood beside her luggage.

"I've never felt so sure about anything in my life, Danny."

"Did you get the new priest settled in?"

"I did."

"I hope he has better luck than his predecessors."

"I'm sure he will."

"So, where will you go in Dublin?"

Dampness settled on them and Fidelma pulled her scarf tighter around her. "I've an aunt there with a large flat who's agreed to take me in."

"What about a job?"

"I'm signing up with a temp agency."

They stood in silence for a moment, watching a

youngster test out his Rollerblades on the main street of Kilkee that sloped down to the seashore.

"Will you miss Ballycara?" Danny asked.

"I will. But then again there's a lot I won't miss. And with Father O'Malley gone ..." her voice trailed off.

"It won't be quite the same, will it?"

"It won't."

"How long have you worked in the rectory?" Danny asked.

"This will be my sixth year."

"Really?" Danny hadn't realized it had been that long. "So you were here when Father Longley died?"

"That's right."

"And the priest before that?"

"I'd been working about a month when Father Bowles passed on." Then, haltingly, "Have you found anything at all yet?"

"I spoke to Chief Superintendent Burke on the phone early this morning. The only prints on the chalice and cruets were Father O'Malley's and Jeremy's."

"What about the bottle of altar wine?"

"Same thing. But something else interesting has turned up. It seems that the folks at the crime lab believe that the combination of poisons found in the bloodstream might have come from a common herbicide."

"You mean the chemical farmers spray on their hayfields to kill weeds?"

"That's right. It appears that someone injected Father with a dose of weed killer."

"Oh, God, this just gets worse every day," she murmured as tears spilled down her cheeks.

Despite the show of grief, Danny wondered why Fidelma was rushing to get out of Ballycara. "The day Father O'Malley died," he began gently, "you were back at the rectory preparing breakfast during Mass."

"I told you that a thousand times."

"You said you served him a cup of tea before Mass."

"Yes."

"Was anyone with you in the rectory?"

"Of course no one was with me. Why in the world—" She stopped and glared at Danny. "What are you trying to say?"

"Nothing, Fidelma, I'm just trying to account for—"

Blood rose in her face and for a moment Danny seriously thought she might hit him. "What are you saying? You want to know if I could have murdered Father O'Malley?" Her voice had taken on an edge of hysteria. "You think I put the sedative into his tea?"

"That's not what I'm saying, Fidelma."

"Is that all the better you've done in your investigation?" Fidelma snapped.

"Well, I have a few ideas. There's something not quite right about this Englishman, Nigel Greene."

"He seems like a perfectly nice man to me," she said, still angry. "I had a long talk with him the day he came to see Father O'Malley at the rectory."

"He went to see Father?" Danny asked, surprised. "What for?"

"I'm not sure, really."

"When was this?"

"A couple days before Father O'Malley died." Fidelma paused for a moment. "You know, I almost forget about that. Greene was in a very good mood. He must have told me a half dozen jokes while he waited for Father O'Malley. But he seemed quite upset when he finished talking with the priest."

"How long was he in with him?"

"About an hour."

"There's something fishy about James Roche, too, if you ask me," Danny said. "He never comes down to eat with the rest of us. Seems to stay in his room all the time. He and his buddy in the blue car almost ran me over. Then I see him out at the site of the peace talks. Who is he, anyway?"

"You're the detective, Danny."

"Look, I'm trying to get to the bottom of this, and now that I'm in the thick of things you're running off to Dublin."

"And that makes me a suspect?"

"What are you talking about, Fidelma? I just asked if there was someone with you before Mass."

"Well, there wasn't."

"Skip it, then. Forget I ever asked."

"Danny," Fidelma began, her tone softened. "I can't tell you how grateful I am that you came down here and found Father for us. I hope you find out who killed him. But I have to get on with my own life now."

Danny's anger subsided as he took a deep breath, held it, then let it out slowly through his nose. "I understand."

He was going to miss Fidelma. But when she moved to Dublin, maybe there'd be a chance that their relationship might develop into something more intimate.

Danny had been chasing Fidelma for the past year as though he was afraid he might catch her. It seems that they'd done nothing but argue since he got to Ballycara. Danny regretted that. He loved her. "Listen," he began, "whatever happens here, I hope we can see each other in Dublin. I'll wait until you get settled."

"Here, Danny," she said, handing him a piece of paper. "Here's my aunt's address and phone number. Call me as soon as you like."

Just then they spotted the bus chugging up the main street. "Well," Danny said awkwardly, "I guess this is it, until I get back to Dublin."

Fidelma's eyes misted as the Bus Eireaan with its trademark Irish setter painted on it stopped in front of them and opened its doors. She fell into Danny's arms. "Goodbye, Danny," she said, and kissed him long and lovingly on the lips. "Thanks for everything."

As she stepped up on the bus she turned and said, "See you in Dublin."

A flock of seagulls glided out toward the cliffs at the edge of town. As Danny watched the bus disappear, he heard a cuckoo call in the distance.

Although it had been a drizzly morning, by late afternoon the sky cleared as Danny walked toward Dr. Cassidy's house outside Ballycara. The sun had broken through a gray mass of clouds moving in from the Atlantic, and the air smelled of rain and turf smoke. Brendan Grady had helped Liam Flynn put up forty bales of hay that they stacked in Liam's field, and the crows screeched from the tops of the yew trees in the graveyard beside St. Bridget's.

Despite the pleasant weather, the news from Chief Superintendent Burke about the fingerprints disappointed Danny. He had hoped they'd find fingerprints that might shed some light on the murder. Nevertheless, the herbicide was an interesting development. Now he wanted to see if Dr. Cassidy could provide any further interpretation of the autopsy report.

On the outskirts of Ballycara, Danny turned up the long shaded drive that led to Dr. Cassidy's newly built ranch-style home. Danny had met Dr. Cassidy on his first visit to Ballycara when he had treated Danny for poisoning. Although he had spoken to him briefly on numerous occasions since then, he didn't know the doctor well.

When Danny rapped on the front door, Mrs. Cassidy greeted him with a smile. "Well, Danny O'Flaherty. Sure, we heard you were back."

"How are you?" Danny asked pleasantly. "Is Doc Cassidy in?"

"He's out back knocking a few hurling balls around. Would you have a cup of tea?"

"No, no. Please don't go to any trouble. I'll just go around back and see the doctor."

Danny found Dr. Cassidy behind the house with a hurling stick in one hand and a half-dozen balls at his feet. He wore a pair of yellow polyester slacks, like one might see on a golf course, and a gray Aran jumper. Despite his gray hair and wrinkles, the elderly doctor was in exceptionally good shape. Hurling, as Danny had first learned from the Irish kids in his neighborhood back in New York, was a Gaelic game somewhat like lacrosse that was played with a broad-bladed stick.

"Danny O'Flaherty," the doctor called good-naturedly as he tossed a ball up in front of him and smacked it out into the pasture behind the house. He offered the hurling stick to Danny. "Will you have a go at it?"

"I'll pass."

"So," said Dr. Cassidy as he flipped another hurling ball up and smashed it deep into the pasture, "I understand you're looking into Father O'Malley's death."

"That's right."

"Tragedy. Terrible tragedy."

"As you know from the autopsy report," Danny said, watching the hurling ball land on the far side of the field, "a variety of poisons were found in Father O'Malley's bloodstream."

"Yes. 'Tis queer. Sure, I've never seen anything like it in all my career."

"I just found out today that these poisons can all be found in herbicide."

"Is that right? Weed killer injected directly into the system would have killed him quickly, I'm sure."

"Yes, and you should have seen the way the body was arranged. It looked as if Father O'Malley had gone to sleep in his vestments. Not a hair on him was disturbed."

"That's because he was sedated before he was injected with the weed killer. With the amount of sedatives they found in his bloodstream, he was probably passed out by the time they shot him with the herbicide."

"That's the way I see it. Someone drugged him,

pushed him down in the basement, then injected the herbicide into him."

"Something like that."

Danny took his copy of the autopsy report from the pocket of his jacket. "This Pethidine ... what is it exactly?"

"Pain killer. It's sold under two trade names: Pethilorfan or Pamergan. In the States I think it's called Demoral. That's how it's normally adminis-tered, anyway."

"Pamergan?" Danny mumbled. Something niggled in the back of his brain.

Dr. Cassidy gripped his hurling stick in his left hand and hefted its weight. "That's about the size of it," he said. "The sedative, alcohol and the poisons were all that was found in the bloodstream. The body itself was unscarred except for the scratches on the hands."

"Defense wounds."

"Aye."

"But how was he given the Demoral? There were no fingerprints on the chalice or the cruets."

Cassidy sent the last ball flying with a smack of the hurling stick. The ball arched over the pasture and disappeared. "There's a good shot," murmured Cassidy. He looked at Danny and shrugged. "I don't know."

They strolled out into the pasture to collect the balls. "How long does it take for this Pethidine to take effect?" Danny asked.

"It acts rather quickly, actually."

"So, it would have to have been given just before

Mass? If it was put in his tea, let's say, at breakfast time ..."

Doctor Cassidy stopped him. "If that much of it was given before Mass, he probably would have passed out during Mass itself."

"I see."

As they searched for the hurling balls, Danny said, "I assume you never prescribed any sedatives for Father O'Malley?"

"I have not been the priest's doctor for over a year now. He has been seeing a doctor in Kilkee."

"But before that, did you prescribe any sedatives?"

"No."

"What is Pamergan usually prescribed for?" Danny spotted one of the balls in the grass and picked it up.

"Severe pain, I'd say offhand."

"Did he have any serious health problems that would warrant a prescription for Pamergan? I mean back when you were treating him?" Danny asked, handing the hurling ball to the doctor.

Dr. Cassidy studied Danny briefly. "Serious?"

"Any problems at all?"

"Nothing that would require pain killers. He had the usual conditions for a man his age. A bladder problem a few years back that turned out to be nothing. I advised him to watch his cholesterol. He liked to eat, you know. Little prostate trouble. Again nothing serious."

Suddenly the niggling stopped. "Did you ever prescribe Pamergan for Peggy Malloy?"

Dr. Cassidy's good humor vanished. "What I do or do not prescribe my patients is strictly confidential." The right corner of his mouth twitched. "Mr. O'Flaherty, what exactly is your interest in Father O'Malley's death?"

"He was my friend. The guys from the pub asked me to find out what I can."

"And you convinced the pathologist to do an autopsy. Congratulations. Really, I mean that. We may have never known what happened to him." Dr. Cassidy forced a smile and held it. "But now, Danny, don't you think it's time you got back to Dublin?"

Danny O'Flaherty appraised the doctor with a certain admiration. The doc got right to the point when he needed to. But why was Dr. Cassidy so anxious to get rid of him? "Everyone was saying Father O'Malley died of a heart attack before I started asking questions. Now, I intend to find out who murdered him," Danny said.

"Why don't you leave it—"

"Yeah, yeah," Danny interrupted. "Leave it to the Garda Siochana. I'll tell you why not. Because Chief Superintendent Burke of the Ennis gardai station asked me to assist him while the guards are busy with the talks in Ennis. I promised him I'd see what I could learn about the priest's death and I intend to do just that."

Doctor Cassidy appeared to relax, then laughed. "Well, good luck to you, sure."

Danny and the doctor gathered the remaining hurling balls and strode back toward the house.

"I understand," Danny began, trying to ease the

coming blow, "that you had a bit of a disagreement with Father O'Malley."

Dr. Cassidy stopped and looked at Danny. "What are you talking about?"

"I'm talking about a woman's right to choose an abortion if she needs one."

"I don't know what you mean."

"Dr. Cassidy, I know you're a man of compassion. That you would try to do the right thing for your patients. I've heard that you've helped more than one girl from the village get to England in order to get around Ireland's abortion laws."

"Mr. O'Flaherty, I'm afraid—"

"And I know that Father O'Malley and you have argued about this in the past. He threatened to turn you in."

"Mr. O'Flaherty, I'm afraid you have overstayed your welcome here. I'm going to have to ask you to leave my property."

Danny handed him the last hurling ball. "Thanks for your time," he said.

Eleven

When Danny knocked at James Roche's door at Shannonside, Roche came to the door frowning. "May I help you?"

Roche wore a three-piece suit and his hair was neatly combed. He had a nervous twitch above his left eye that made his eyebrow jump. Dandruff sprinkled the shoulders of his jacket, and the hairs in his nose needed trimming.

"I hope so," said Danny. "I'd like to have a word with you, Mr. Roche."

Roche examined Danny from head to foot. "I'm on my way out."

"It won't take a second."

A man of about fifty-five, Roche had lost some hair on top and gray dappled the sides. His skin had a sallow hue and the dark bags under his eyes made him look like he had not slept well for some time. "I don't believe we've met," he said.

"Name's Danny O'Flaherty," Danny said, extending his hand.

Roche considered the proffered hand as if it were

a dead fish, but finally took it and gave it a limp shake. "I've really got to go," he said. "I'm supposed to meet somebody; I can only spare a moment."

"I was just wondering," Danny said casually, "what you know about Father O'Malley's last Mass."

Roche's head snapped back as though he'd been slapped. After an interval of silence, he recovered. "I'm not sure I know what you're talking about."

"You were at Mass the morning Father O'Malley was murdered."

"Yes?"

"I understand you were also in the sacristy."

"Who said I was in the sacristy?"

"Jeremy Malloy," Danny said.

Roche creased his forehead. "Jeremy Malloy?"

"The altar boy. He saw you talk to the priest."

"Did he?"

"I was just wondering what you wanted to see him about?"

"I'm not sure that is something that would concern you, Mr. O'—" Roche searched for the name.

"O'Flaherty," Danny said. "And I think it does concern me. May I come in?"

"You may not," said Roche, blocking the door.

Danny and James Roche glared at each other for a moment. Then Roche said, "I had a private matter to discuss with him."

"And he was too busy to talk with you?"

"That's right."

"Mind telling me what sort of matter?"

"Yes, I do mind. I said it was private."

"Mr. Roche," Danny said, "you were one of the last people to see Father O'Malley alive. If there's anything you can tell me, I'd appreciate it."

James Roche opened the door wider and Danny could see the interior of his room.

"I went to see Father O'Malley about," Roche faltered slightly, "a spiritual matter. The priest was in a hurry, so I said I'd speak to him another time."

"Was this before or after Mass?"

"Mr. O'Flaherty, I'm late."

Danny noticed something on the table inside the room that caught his eye—three bottles of medicine and a syringe. "The altar boy said he saw a blue car after Mass that was parked near the cemetery, as if waiting for someone. Did you see it, by any chance?"

Roche furrowed his brow. "No, I didn't see any car."

"Do you know anybody with a blue car?"

"Mr. O'Flaherty, I've lived in this village less than three weeks. I don't know anybody with a blue or any other color car."

"A Peugot?"

"I'm afraid I must be going."

Roche saw Danny looking in the direction of the table, and as if reading Danny's thoughts said, "I don't know what you're thinking, but I have diabetes. If you must know, I have to give myself insulin shots." James Roche's left eye twitched and he breathed in short gasps, as if the wind had been knocked from him.

Then, without another word, he closed the door in Danny's face.

Danny went out the front entrance of Shannonside, crossed the street, and crouched in the doorway of Larkin's Pub.

"What are you doing?"

Danny whirled around, his heart thumping, and faced Tim Mahoney.

"You scared me," Danny whispered, then put his finger to his lips and made a motion with his other hand for Tim to keep moving.

Tim went into the pub, shaking his head and mumbling.

Danny saw Roche come out of the bed and breakfast, turn north, and walk briskly up the main street of Ballycara. Danny followed him through the village. The sky had darkened and threatened to storm again. But Roche seemed oblivious to it. He passed the church and the rectory, then stepped off the road over a narrow canal into a hayfield.

Danny trailed him to the back of the field near a cluster of whitethorn trees. Under the shade of the trees stood a circle of stones among the overgrown grass. Danny hid behind a tree. To the west, he could see the rectory.

Roche glanced around, as if expecting someone. Danny ducked behind the tree, making a conscious effort to get his breathing back to normal. When at last he peeked out again, Roche had set off across the field in the direction of the rectory; Danny followed. They skirted the priest's residence, crossed the main road of Ballycara again, and cut through the side yard of a small home, over a stone fence and into the back pasture of a farm. In the distance, Danny could see another circle of whitethorn trees at the edge of the •field. The ring forts.

Danny had laughed when Tim Mahoney spoke of the curse of the ring forts. "You sound to me like you believe there *is* a path for the fairies there," Danny had said.

"Well, it's not a matter of whether I believe it. What *does* matter is that no good has ever come to a priest who's lived in that rectory."

As Danny watched Roche, he spotted a car approaching across the field on a little-used road that he had not even noticed. The car was a Peugot—blue—the same one he had seen Roche get out of the other night, and had seen at the site of the peace talks in Ennis.

So, Roche doesn't know anyone with a blue car, eh? Danny thought.

Roche approached the car as it stopped. A tall, gangly man in a white shirt, tie, and sports jacket got out and shook hands with him. Danny dropped to his hands and knees and crawled behind one of the massive boulders of the ring fort, then concealed himself in a crevice between two stones.

"I'm not safe here anymore," Danny heard Roche tell the man.

"Why not?"

"There's this American in town playing private detective."

Danny's pulse quickened. He lay with his face pressed to the ground behind the stone. A blade of grass tickled his nose.

"Trying to find out who killed the priest?"

"Exactly."

"So what does he know?"

"Not much. But he's asking a lot of questions."

Danny pulled the grass away from his face and scratched his nose.

"I'm afraid he's going to stumble onto something sooner or later," Roche continued. "I've got to get out of here."

"Can you sit tight for a while longer?"

"I tell you he's going to blow the whole thing wide open. He's asking everybody in the village all these questions."

Danny felt a prickly sensation begin in his nose.

"Look," the man in the white shirt began, "we've gone to a lot of trouble and expense here. You've got to sit tight."

The prickly sensation grew.

"But I'm telling you," Roche said, his voice rising, "if he starts digging into what I'm doing in Ballycara he's going to find me out."

Danny pinched his nose with his thumb and forefinger.

"I think you're getting scared without reason. You said yourself he knows nothing."

"Not now he doesn't. But he knows I went to see the priest before Mass."

"So what? I say let's sit on it for a while."

"I can't."

Danny let out an explosive sneeze.

"What was that?" the man in the white shirt asked.

He flipped the tail of his sports jacket away and put his hand on the butt of a revolver in a holster on his waist.

James Roche looked around. "I don't know."

Danny saw the man in the jacket slowly remove the gun from his waist and glance around the ring fort.

Danny drew his body up into a ball and squeezed himself deeper into the crevice.. *Oh my God*, he thought, *they're going to kill me.*

"Let's get out of here," Roche said uneasily.

Danny peered around the stone and saw the man with the gun walking toward him as he swept the gun in an arc around the ring fort. "Maybe it's one of those fairies you were telling me about," he said. "You said there was a curse on this place, didn't you?" he added, laughing.

"Stop your messing and let's go. I'm the one who's in a bind here," said Roche.

The other man pulled the hammer back on his gun and pointed it toward Danny's hiding place. "Maybe I could kill me a leprechaun while I'm down here, what do you think?"

Danny nearly pissed his pants. This guy was nuts, and if he found him, he'd shoot him on sight.

"Jesus Christ, man, have you gone 'round the bend? Let's go."

"Yeah, I could blast me a leprechaun and bring him back to Dublin. Maybe have him stuffed."

Sweat had broken out on Danny's forehead and a bead of it dripped into his left eye. The burning in his eye gave him an odd relief from his terror.

"Are you out of your mind?"

The man with the gun laughed maniacally. "The curse of the bloody ring forts. These people down here are a bunch of *culchies*."

"Let's get out of here," Roche said.

"No," the man answered, walking around the area, pointing the gun up a tree, on the ground, behind him. "I heard something."

Danny held his breath and began a silent Act of Contrition.

"Come on," said Roche, "it was nothing."

"You're too jumpy," the man said. He stepped around the stone and Danny could practically see into the little holes on the front of his wingtip shoes. "If I kill me a leprechaun, I'll share the crock of gold with you."

"We're wasting time," Roche shouted. "The American is back there right now finding out everything he can about me."

The man took another step. "Maybe I'll kill me an American, too, while I'm at it."

Danny squeezed his eyes shut when the man asked, "What's that?"

Danny opened his eyes. The man walked a short distance, leaned over, and picked a wallet off the ground.

Danny reached around and felt his back pocket. He must have dropped it when he was climbing behind the boulder.

"Well, well," the man said. "My crock of gold."

"Come on, dammit," said Roche moving toward the car.

The man looked inside. "It's your man's wallet. Hey, Danny O'Flaherty!" he called in a singsong voice, pointing the gun toward the ring fort. "You dropped your wallet."

Roche jumped behind the wheel of the car and started the engine. "I'm getting out of here," he said. "Are you coming?"

The other man eased the hammer down on the gun, dropped the wallet on the ground, climbed into the blue car, and they sped away.

After Danny's breathing had returned to normal and his racing heart had calmed, he stood on shaking legs, brushed himself off, and clambered from inside the crevice. He picked up his wallet, and started back toward Shannonside when his eye caught something hanging from one of the whitethorn trees.

"What the hell?" Danny murmured as he approached it.

The body of a black-and-white house cat hung from a length of rope. A noose had been tied around the cat's throat, and its tongue stuck out through its bared teeth.

Danny stared a moment before he untied the rope from the tree and lowered the cat's stiff body gently to the ground. A similar thing had happened recently in Limerick. Devil worshippers had sacrificed a cat in a ring fort on May Eve. Was this part of the Midsummer rite?

Danny raced back out to the main road, reaching it as Desmond Conlon came by on a bicycle.

"Did you see two men in a blue car?" Danny asked.

Desmond nodded.

"Which way did they go?"

Desmond pointed in the direction of the village.

As Danny burst through the door of the bed and breakfast, Mrs. Slattery looked up from *Fair City* on the telly. "My Lord," she said as she got up, "what's wrong?"

He strode across the living room and banged on the door to Roche's room. "Open up, Roche!"

"What is it?" asked Mrs. Slattery from behind Danny.

"Roche killed Father O'Malley," said Danny as he banged again on the door. "Open up!"

"God help us," said Mrs. Slattery, blessing herself.

"Do you have the key to the room?" Danny asked as he pulled on the knob.

"I'll get it."

Mrs. Slattery returned with the key and Danny opened the door. Inside, the closets had been cleaned out. All that had been left behind were a few coat-hangers, an *Irish Times* with an article on Father O'Malley's murder, and a couple empty stout bottles.

"When did he leave?"

"I didn't even notice he was leaving. I just got back from Carmody's shop."

"Where's your car?"

"Around back," said Mrs. Slattery.

A schedule of Brittany Ferries from Cork, on the night-table near the bed, caught Danny's eye. He snatched it up. The ferry from Cork to St. Malo, France, had been circled. It would leave Cork at 19:00; in just three hours.

"Does Roche have a car?" Danny asked, not sure if Roche had left with the man in the blue car or taken his own.

"Sure he does; it's around back, parked right beside mine."

Danny threw open the window and craned his neck to see into the back yard. "Where's his car?" he asked Mrs. Slattery again.

"It's right back there," she said, putting her own head out the window. Then she drew in a quick breath. "It's gone."

Mrs. Slattery pulled her head back inside.

Danny slammed the window closed and started out of the room. "I guess Mr. Roche has decided on a little vacation in France."

Twelve

"I'm going after him," said Danny. "Can I use your car?"

"I'll go with you." Mrs. Slattery put on a hat and coat and fetched her purse.

"Are you sure?"

"I've to put on a bit of lipstick first."

"Mrs. Slattery, please ..."

"'Twill only take a second."

Danny sighed.

When Mrs. Slattery finished, they sped out of Ballycara in her Ford Fiesta, passed Desmond on his bicycle, and picked up the Kilrush Road in Kilkee, headed for the Killimer car ferry.

"The ferry crosses the Shannon to Tarbert in County Kerry," Mrs. Slattery explained. "If we catch the ferry, we can connect with Cork without having to go back around the River Shannon through Limerick. Then we can pick up N-20 near Buttevant or Mallow, and head south through Mourne Abbey, Blarney, and into Cork."

"Do what?" Danny asked.

"Never mind," said Mrs. Slattery. "Just turn where I tell you."

As he drove, Danny told Mrs. Slattery what had happened at the ring fort.

"But what made you follow him there to begin with?" she asked.

He explained about Jeremy Malloy seeing a blue car waiting outside the church after Mass, and that he himself had seen Roche talking to a man in a blue car the first night he was in the village. Then he had seen Roche get out of a blue Peugot at the Old Ground Hotel. And Jeremy had said that Roche went in to the sacristy to see Father O'Malley before Mass. To top it off, he had seen a hypodermic needle in Roche's room. "Did you know he was diabetic?" Danny asked.

"No."

"That's what he claims to be; I don't believe it. The way I see it," Danny continued, "Roche put the Demoral in the cruet of wine before Mass and Father O'Malley drank it at the consecration of the host. By the time Mass was over, Father O'Malley could barely stand. Roche went to the sacristy, opened the door to the cellar, led Father down, laid him out, and finished him with the final shot. Walked up, locked the door behind him, slipped out of the sacristy, and back to Shannonside."

"But why? Why did he do it?"

"I'm not sure. Maybe he's in some kind of devil worshipping cult that's going around killing Catholic priests."

"What?"

"You see, after Roche and his accomplice left, I found a cat hanging by its neck from a tree inside the ring fort."

"The Lord have mercy on us," she said, blessing herself.

"I think it was Jeremy Malloy's cat. They told me it was missing."

"There hasn't been an ounce of luck in this parish since they built that rectory. You're *sure* this Mr. Roche murdered Father O'Malley?"

"Positive. And you should have heard the guy he was with. A real sicko; talking about wasting leprechauns."

"And to think he was living under my own roof. My God! He was such a cheerless fellow. Gloomy and gruff. I always knew he was a bad one."

Danny took the curves on the narrow Kilrush road at high speed. Mrs. Slattery emitted a high-pitched "Lord have mercy," when they took a turn too sharply and the back of the Ford fishtailed.

Suddenly, she screamed and covered her eyes. "My God, look out!"

Danny tried to put the brake pedal through the floorboard as they screeched to a halt inches in front of a herd of sheep. "Close one," he said as he eased the car through the pack of animals. "Almost had lamb chops for dinner."

Mrs. Slattery blessed herself.

Danny figured Roche could not have been on the road too long; there was still a chance to catch him if he pulled off for petrol or slowed down. Danny held the accelerator to the floor for a good thirty miles of rolling pastureland.

They made the car ferry just in time.

"You know, now that I think of it," Mrs. Slattery said as they chugged across the Shannon on the car ferry, "he had the eyes of a murderer. I had an aunt who could tell a person's fate by looking in his eyes. I've a bit of the gift meself."

"That right?" Danny said, thinking, too bad you didn't use your gift to prevent Father O'Malley's murder.

"Oh yes," she murmured, then suddenly said, "I wonder was Mr. Roche born on Pentecost? Sure, my aunt used to say that a person born on Pentecost was either fated to kill or be killed."

"Maybe it was Father O'Malley who was born on Pentecost," said Danny.

"I think he was!"

When they reached the other side of the Shannon, they drove off the ferry into County Kerry. Soon, Danny pulled up behind a green Volvo.

"Is that his car?" he asked anxiously, having no idea what Roche drove.

"Indeed, it is."

Danny shifted into fourth gear and raced after the Volvo. The driver in front accelerated, but Danny stayed on him. He downshifted at a sharp turn, then shot through an open straightaway flanked by small farms, hayfields, and scattered homes.

Up ahead the road curved through low hills, and puddles of water stood in the pockmarked surface of the pavement. Danny kept the accelerator down until they reached Mourne Abbey, where rain began to splatter the windshield.

The road grew slick, and Danny pulled back on his speed. He flipped on the wipers and searched for Roche's taillights in the mist ahead. Once he reached France, Roche would probably stay out of sight for a month or two. After things cooled down he could re-enter Ireland or go back to Australia.

Danny downshifted, and drove on through the rain. Water pounded on the roof of the car and visibility was down to ten feet at best. The wind blew broken branches from the trees across the road and Danny maneuvered around them.

"Did we lose him?" Mrs. Slattery asked, squinting ahead.

"He's had to slow down, too. We'll catch him."

"Then what?" she asked, her eyes gleaming with an unfamiliar light.

Indeed, then what? Danny had no weapon. He had his fists, but was not inclined to use them. "We'll think of something," he replied. He checked his watch: almost six o'clock. The ferry would leave Cork at seven.

Soon the rain slackened and Danny made up time as he rocketed through the green countryside.

Suddenly, Mrs. Slattery yelled, "There he is," and pointed ahead.

Danny sped after him, and Roche glanced at them in the rearview. As Danny eased behind him, a bottle flew out of the driver's side and smashed on the road in front of them. Danny swerved violently, then brought the car back under control. Another bottle hit the Fiesta where the roof joined the windshield. A spiderweb of shattered glass formed at the top of the windshield on Mrs. Slattery's side, but it stayed in one piece.

"Oh," Mrs. Slattery squeaked.

"Son-of-a-bitch," Danny muttered as he threw the gear into fifth.

"Danny," Mrs. Slattery said gently, "watch your language."

Danny drew up within a couple feet of the back of the car. He could see Roche glancing rapidly from the road to the rearview mirror. Danny accelerated and gently nudged the back of Roche's car with the bumper of Mrs. Slattery's. Another bottle grazed Danny's side mirror and caromed off into the grass beside the road.

"My God," gasped Mrs. Slattery. "He'll kill us."

"Bullshit," Danny muttered, then glanced sideways. "Sorry." Danny drew up alongside Roche, then jerked the wheel violently to the left.

"Be careful," yelled Mrs. Slattery. Danny didn't know if she was fearful for her life or her car.

The impact drove Roche onto the shoulder, but he kept his car under control and pulled back onto the road. Danny swerved again, and his front bumper shattered the headlight on the driver's side of Roche's car.

Roche hurled something else from the window.

"My God," cried Mrs. Slattery, "that's the comforter I knitted last year. He must have taken it from the room."

The blanket unfurled in mid-air, snagged on the corner of the hood, and spread out across the windshield.

"Jesus Christ," Danny muttered, thrusting his head out the window.

Mrs. Slattery furrowed her brow. "We mustn't take the Lord's name in vain, Danny."

Danny tugged at the blanket and lost control of the car. He whipped the steering wheel to the left and pulled the car back onto the road. "Hold the wheel," he yelled.

Mrs. Slattery slid over and grasped the steering wheel with both hands while Danny pulled at the blanket.

"I can't see a thing," yelled Mrs. Slattery.

The comforter was not only snagged on the hood but wound round the antenna as well.

"Careful not to tear it," Mrs. Slattery called.

Roche had shot another half-mile ahead of them and Danny floored it. The comforter flapped and popped against the windshield while Mrs. Slattery struggled to untangle it from the antenna. Suddenly it broke free and Mrs. Slattery yelped as it rose from the windshield, nearly taking her arm with it, and sailed onto the road behind them.

"It took six months to make that," she muttered.

Danny had drawn up so close behind Roche that he could see his sallow face in his rearview mirror.

Suddenly, Roche veered to the left onto a secondary road. Danny jammed the brake down and turned after Roche, but the tires lost their grip on the wet road and the car spun out of control. Danny felt helpless as the car spun around once in a counter-clockwise motion, then once again. He looked over at Mrs. Slattery, whose lips had formed a perfect and soundless "O." The car slid off the road and stopped with a jolt, facing the opposite direction.

Danny rested his head on the steering wheel and took a deep breath. His hands shook as he gripped the wheel. "You okay?" he asked.

Mrs. Slattery's lips and jaws moved but no sound came out.

"Are you all right?" Danny asked again.

She nodded, her mouth still silently working.

"Good," Danny said, putting the car into first and easing back onto the highway. He found the road where Roche had turned and followed him. The car made an odd ticking noise.

Danny shifted into high gear and shot after Roche. Within a few miles they drew up behind him again. The ticking beneath the car had escalated to a ratcheting, and a wisp of steam seeped from beneath the hood. Danny watched the temperature gauge climb, and silently prayed that the car would hold together.

"Here, take over," he said as he pulled the car to the side of the road, put the gear in neutral, and ran around to the passenger side.

Mrs. Slattery climbed into the driver's seat.

"Let's go," said Danny.

Mrs. Slattery took off, the ratcheting sound still coming from beneath the car.

She certainly knew her way around an automobile, Danny noted. She closed the distance between the cars within a few miles. When they were behind Roche again, Danny rolled down the window. "Pull up beside him."

Mrs. Slattery eased around the Volvo. Danny saw Roche lick his lips nervously as they drew up beside him.

"Keep your speed steady," Danny shouted, and began climbing out of the passenger side.

"What are you doing?"

"Just keep your speed even with his."

Danny sat on the door, his feet in the passenger seat.

"Be careful, for God's sake."

He steadied himself on the roof as he swung one leg out of the window. Mrs. Slattery pulled up beside Roche, who flew along at over fifty miles per hour. Danny stretched his right foot toward the open window of Roche's car. Suddenly, Mrs. Slattery swerved and the two cars separated, nearly spilling Danny onto the road, then came together again, nearly crushing him between them.

"Watch what you're doing," Danny screamed.

"Do *you* want to drive?" Mrs. Slattery screamed back, shoving her glasses farther up on her nose.

Roche increased his speed, but Mrs. Slattery stuck to him like a loyal dog. Danny shoved one foot in Roche's window, one hand on the doorframe, and attempted to pull himself into Roche's car.

But Roche stomped on the accelerator. Danny began to be slowly and excruiatingly wrenched apart.

"Speed up," Danny yelled to Mrs. Slattery.

"What?" She cupped a hand behind her ear.

"Speed up, for Christ's sake," Danny managed.

"I told you to watch your tongue!" She shook a finger at him.

Roche smirked sadistically as Danny's legs spread wider and wider, clinging to the car.

The ratcheting beneath the hood had become a grinding screech, and clouds of hot steam and spray billowed from under the hood, singeing Danny's face. He struggled to pull himself into Roche's car but Roche pounded Danny's hands as he clung to the window frame.

Mrs. Slattery's car began to drop behind.

"Speed up," Danny shouted as his fingers slipped on Roche's car.

Mrs. Slattery continued to lose speed. As Danny lost his grip, the pavement rose up toward him. He tried to disentangle his leg and climb back into Mrs. Slattery's car. "What's wrong?" he screamed.

"We're losing power."

"Bugger off, Yank!" James Roche yelled as Danny pulled his leg out of the window of Roche's car and dropped to within inches of the pavement, clinging to Mrs. Slattery's side mirror. Steam spewed out of the radiator, and deposited a spray of rust-colored mist across the windscreen.

Danny hung upside down, his head almost scraping the ground, but he could still see the back of Roche's car disappear ahead.

The Fiesta slowed, hiccoughed, backfired twice, and finally came to a shuddering halt in the road. The engine gave off a high-pitched ping, belched, and shut down as if exhausted. "Shit!" Mrs. Slattery shouted, pounding the steering wheel.

Smoke curled from under the hood as Danny released himself and dropped to the ground. "Watch your tongue," he said sourly.

"We almost had him!"

Danny's pulse hammered. He stood up and opened the hood of the car and Mrs. Slattery came around to see. Danny touched the engine block. "Ouch," he yelped, and jerked his hand back.

"He got away," Mrs. Slattery added desultorily, staring after the long-gone Volvo. But her eyes were glowing. She finally focused on Danny. "So, are you all right, then?"

A salesman of bottled water stopped and gave them a lift to the ferry in Cork. Danny looked back at Mrs. Slattery's still smoking Fiesta and prayed she had good insurance.

At the ferry landing in Cork, Danny and Mrs. Slattery jumped out of the water salesman's car and ran toward the docks. James Roche's green Volvo sat abandoned beside the dock. Two hundred yards offshore, the St. Malo ferry chugged out to open sea.

"He's getting away," Mrs. Slattery said. "Let's see if we can hire a boat and go after him."

Danny shook his head. "I don't think so. I've already wrecked your car." She expected him to rent a boat? "Let's just cut our losses. I'll call Burke and have Roche picked up on the other side."

After Danny left a message for the superintendent, Mrs. Slattery called for a tow-truck in Cork to haul her car back to Ballycara where she would have Desmond Conlon take a look at it. Then Danny O'Flaherty and Breda Slattery sat in the cab, beside the tow-truck driver, in absolute silence on the long ride back to Ballycara.

Thirteen

Danny walked into Larkin's Pub the next day in a mood for neither *craic* nor cod. He had spent all night going over the events of the disastrous chase to the Cork ferry and berating himself—how could he have let Roche get away?

By the time Roche landed in St. Malo, Chief Superintendent Burke would have alerted the *gendarme* in France that Roche had boarded the ferry and could be apprehended on that side. Which was fine, considering how Danny had boggled the chase.

Meanwhile, Mrs. Slattery had contacted Desmond Conlon about her car, and the news was not good. Desmond would have to replace the head gasket, which was not a problem in itself, he explained in his own awkward way. But in order to get to the head he would have to pull the engine out of the car.

"Big job," Desmond had said.

It seemed Danny would be teaching summer school for the rest of his life in order to pay for the damages. Either that or he'd quit his teaching job in Dublin altogether, go back to New York, and take up his father's trade at the O'Flaherty Funeral Parlor.

Inside Larkin's Pub, Seamus Larkin stood behind the bar with a two-day old *Irish Times* open in front of him, and stared up at the telly. Tim Mahoney sat alone nursing his stout near the fire.

"So," Seamus called as Danny entered the pub, "look who's back from France. Congratulations!"

"I didn't go to France," Danny said bitterly.

"Why not? Sure, you could have done some damage to the ferry as well."

Tim Mahoney guffawed. "He's just codding you. We heard you found the killer. Good work!"

"What's your poison?" Larkin asked.

Danny studied the publican for a moment, not sure he approved of his word choice. "Give me a Harp," Danny said, "and a shot of Bushmills with it."

"It's on the house, Danny Boy."

Just then Brendan Grady came in. He had dyed his mohawk again, a fluorescent green.

"Good Lord in heaven," Larkin said when he saw Grady. "What in God's name will you do to yourself next?"

Brendan ran his hand fondly over his mohawk. He also had another hole pierced in his ear and sported a new silver ring.

"The things he's picking up in Galway," Larkin mumbled.

"I like it," said Tim Mahoney.

"Does it glow in the dark?" asked the publican.

Danny took his pint over to where Tim sat by the turf fire, which barely kept the dampness out of the room. Danny sipped his Harp and gazed at the flames.

By now the French police would have arrested Roche in St. Malo.

"We're grateful you found the murderer," Brendan said after he'd gotten his pint of Guinness. "Tell us how you figured out it was James Roche."

Danny turned to Brendan. "It was really just a matter of motive and opportunity." He took a sip of his Harp. "You see, Father O'Malley's final Mass had ended at 10:30. If someone from the church followed him (or forced him) into the basement after Mass and killed him, they would have taken his keys from his belt, then locked the door to the basement on the way out."

The door of the pub rattled open and Liam Flynn stepped inside. He removed his hat and put it down carefully on a chair. "Pint o'Guinness," he said to the publican.

Larkin drew the pint for the elderly villager and set it in front of him on the bar. Liam picked up his Guinness, took a deep gulp and set it down in front of him. "Ah," he said, smacking his lips, "thank God you found out who did it. I'm after hearing the story from Breda Slattery. I never did like that man, Roche."

"Once the autopsy revealed that a sedative had been found in Father O'Malley's bloodstream," Danny continued, "I figured that someone had slipped into the sacristy and dropped a heavy dose of it into the Communion wine. Father O'Malley drank the wine at the consecration of the host, about midway through Mass. By the time Mass was over, he could barely stand. That much I figured out. But who had the opportunity?"

Liam Flynn cleared his throat and took his pipe from the pocket of his jacket.

"Only James Roche," Danny concluded, "had the opportunity to drop the sedative in the Communion wine. Jeremy Malloy saw him go into the sacristy before Mass. He also saw someone in a blue car waiting outside the church. On two separate occasions I saw Roche talking to someone in a blue car. Later, Roche told me he didn't know anyone with a blue car. Well, I figured he must have put the sedative into the wine, then after Mass he went into the sacristy, forced Father O'Malley down into the cellar, and shot him with the herbicide. Later, I saw the syringe in his room, as well as some bottles of medicine, and put two and two together."

"That bastard," Liam mumbled. "May he rot in hell!"

"But what about the cat?" asked Tim.

"Well, that's connected to the motive. You see, I think Roche and his accomplice are in some kind of devil worshipping cult that is into sacrificing cats and Catholic priests."

"Bloody hell!"

"But it wasn't until I saw the syringe in James Roche's room that I knew he was the killer," Danny concluded. "That's why I followed him out to the ring fort. I heard him tell the man in the blue car that if I kept asking questions I was going to find him out. Well, little did he know I had already found him out." Danny sat back with a satisfied smile.

"Well done," Liam said.

The midday news came on telly and Seamus reached up and turned up the volume. "Today's top story involves a bizarre new twist in the murder of Father Padraic O'Malley of St. Bridget's parish, Ballycara, County Clare."

"Here comes your fifteen minutes of fame, Dan," said Brendan, pulling his chair up for a better view of the telly.

"Our crime reporter, Paul Reynolds, has the story. Paul."

"An arrest was made this morning in St. Malo, France, as a result of a tip phoned in to Chief Superintendent Lawrence Burke of the gardai station in Ennis."

"A tip," Danny said good-naturedly. "I practically caught him myself." Despite the fact that the guards would get all the credit for the arrest, it was still clear to everyone in the pub, and in the village, that it was Danny who had done all the legwork and Danny who had solved the crime. Even so, as long as Father O'Malley's killer was being brought to justice, it didn't really matter who took credit for it.

"A Mr. James Roche of Ballycara," the reporter continued, "was picked up in St. Malo as soon as he got off the ferry from Cork."

"So, they got him," Danny said.

"When he was returned to Ireland for an arraignment this morning, it was learned that James Roche is very important to the Garda Siochana."

"I guess he is," Danny said.

"About twenty years ago," the reporter continued, "James Roche was a key witness in the government's case against an organized crime group in Dublin."

"You hear that?" Danny asked, "he's mixed up in organized crime, too." Danny took another sip of his pint.

"According to sources within Dublin Castle, Roche

was a high-ranking official in the special branch of the Garda Siochana when he testified against three organized crime figures in Dublin. There were threats made against his life."

Danny stared at the telly, a sick feeling beginning to overtake him.

"When the Garda Siochana no longer believed they could guarantee his safety in Ireland, he was given a generous sum of money, a special commendation for service above and beyond the call of duty, and relocated to Australia where he has lived as a private citizen for the past nineteen years."

"But—" Danny began.

"Until last year when they thought it was safe to bring him back to Ireland. Apparently, the government witness suffers from diabetes and wanted to come home. He was given a new identity, a handsome salary, and he retired to the small West of Ireland village of Ballycara."

"You mean—"

"Where he has lived quietly for the past month," the reporter went on, "until an American, acting on behalf of the local gardai chased him out of the country, believing he was the murderer of the parish priest."

"Oh no," Danny gasped.

"Sources in Dublin are saying that the cover has been blown off the most highly protected and respected government witness in the history of the Republic of Ireland."

"Huh?" Danny squeaked.

Seamus Larkin sneered.

"James Roche's real name is Donovan Quinn. He

was responsible for the arrest and conviction of three of the biggest crime figures to have ever operated in Ireland. His identity has been a carefully—and expensively—guarded secret."

Larkin looked at Danny and laughed. "O'Flaherty, your man Roche had absolutely nothing to do with the death of Father O'Malley. I'm afraid that was all an elaborate fabrication on your part—codology, as we say in Ireland."

"But he ran," Danny said feebly. "He ran away."

As if hearing Danny's comment, the anchor asked: "Paul, why did Donovan Quinn attempt to flee the country?"

"He had little choice, Ann," said the reporter. "At first he thought that the man chasing him was part of the crime ring that has been trying to get to him for all these years. Later, he realized that he had been mistaken for the murderer of the parish priest."

"This can't be happening ..." Danny began.

"And he decided to run before his cover was blown completely," the anchor added.

"Your man in the blue car," Larkin said, "must have been an agent as well."

"Probably assigned to protect Roche until he was fully integrated into the community," Tim added.

"My God," Liam Flynn gasped.

"This is just the latest bizarre twist in what is turning out to be a highly unusual murder investigation," the reporter wound up his report. "At this point, the murderer of Father O'Malley is still at large, and

Donovan Quinn will be relocated once again and given a new identity. Back to you, Ann."

Seamus Larkin chuckled as he drew a fresh round of stouts.

Danny dropped his head into his hands.

"Well," Larkin said, snapping off the telly with a remote. "I have two words of advice for you, Danny. I suggest you listen carefully."

"But I—"

"Two words," said Larkin.

"I'm listening," said Danny, defeated.

Larkin smiled. "Go home."

Fourteen

Danny looked around the pub sheepishly. Maybe it *was* time to go home. He took off his glasses and rubbed his face with both hands. The strain of the last couple days was getting to him. He wished Fidelma were here.

"Don't take it so hard," Brendan said, carrying a fresh pint of Guinness to where Danny sat by the fire. "We'll find out who did it."

Seamus Larkin said, "Like I said, don't you think maybe it's time to go home?"

"But we're the ones who asked Danny to look into this," Brendan said. "How can you tell him now to go home? If not Danny, then who is to find the killer of Father O'Malley?"

"I say leave it to the Garda Siochana."

"I've been hearing that," said Danny, "since the day I got here."

"Besides," added Brendan, "the guards won't have a man down here for a week."

"That's right."

"Danny," Larkin leaned across the bar. "You took your best shot. Let it go, lad."

Danny held Larkin's gaze for a moment, then sipped his Harp. "Aren't you curious about who killed Father O'Malley, Seamus?" Danny asked.

Larkin wiped the bar in long, even circles. "Of course I am. I'm just thinking it may be beyond our ken to ever know."

Danny dropped his head into his hands again. If Roche didn't do it, then who was left? There were eight people at Mass—nine, including the altar boy—the day Father O'Malley was murdered. Since Father O'Malley apparently never left the church after Mass, Danny reflected, it must have been someone who was at Mass who killed him, then dragged him down into the cellar. Numerous theories presented themselves—devil worshippers, Protestant extremists from Northern Ireland, IRA members trying to disrupt the talks in Ennis, the curse on the rectory—but who in the village could he connect to these theories?

Danny stole a glance at Liam Flynn, who sucked on his pipe as he related to Brendan, for the fiftieth time, the way in which the Loop Head Peninsula had gotten its name. "You see, in Irish it means Leap Head. The great Cuchulain was running away from a witch who was trying to seduce him. The witch's name was Mal. Well, you see Cuchulain leapt from the cliffs to those rocks offshore called Diarmuid and Grainne's Rocks to try to get away from the witch. Well, didn't the witch do the same thing. So Cuchulain leapt back to the mainland. When the witch tried to leap back she fell short and plummeted into the channel. Sure, didn't the current sweep her body up north to a bay.

That's why the bay up near Spanish Point is called
Mal Bay. And this peninsula we live on here is called
the Loop Head Peninsula."

"Fascinating," Brendan said, stiffling a yawn.

Flynn had been at Mass that morning. In fact,
according to Mrs. Slattery, he had been first in line
for Communion. As far as weed killer, a farmer like
Liam probably had gallons of it in his barn. But he
couldn't picture Liam dragging the priest down into
the basement. Unless he had an accomplice.

Brendan Grady? The mystery man of Ballycara.
No one seemed to know what he did in Galway. Then
there were his alleged IRA connections. It was odd
that he had never once mentioned the talks in Ennis
after that first time. Brendan was not at Mass that
morning, or any other morning as far as Danny knew.
With his fluorescent green mohawk and earrings,
Brendan wouldn't have been overlooked.

"Tell me," Danny said to Liam Flynn, "what exactly was it that Breda Slattery disagreed with Father
O'Malley about?"

Liam took his pipe from his mouth and chortled.
"Ever since the Second Vatican Council, Breda Slattery
has argued with every priest who's come to Ballycara.
She has never adjusted to the changes in the Church.
As far as she's concerned we should still be saying
Mass in Latin and not eating meat on Fridays."

Danny remembered Mrs. Slattery say that Father
O'Malley was not the easiest person to get along with.
Maybe it was the other way around. "That's it?"

"That was enough," said Liam. He put his pipe down,

took a long pull from his stout, and wiped his mouth with a handkerchief he took from his back pocket. "She worried poor Father O'Malley to death every time he tried to change something. Once some of the young folks wanted to have a folk Mass with guitars and what-not. Good Lord, listening to Breda Slattery tell it you'd think he wanted to invite the devil to Mass."

Was that all there was to it? During the chase to Cork, she seemed mighty anxious to catch Roche and hang the murder on him. She actually wanted to hire a boat and go after the ferry. She didn't know Roche was a protected witness and maybe she thought it would be convenient if the murder charges stuck to him. She certainly had the opportunity to kill the priest, since she was at Mass. Besides, hadn't he seen her using herbicide in her garden? Maybe Breda Slattery was not who Danny thought she was.

"What about Dr. Cassidy?" Danny asked. Of all the villagers, he certainly had the means to commit the crime. He could easily get sedatives and would have access to a syringe. Although not at Mass the morning Father O'Malley was murdered, it was well known he had disagreed with the priest.

"Well, now," Brendan said, "Father O'Malley practically excommunicated the doctor from the Church. To be honest with you, I think the priest was unfair to him."

"Unfair?" Liam said, his voice rising. "The man had a hand in helping young girls ..." Liam's voice trailed off, then in a whisper he added, "It's a mortal sin."

"Mortal sin?" Brendan shot back. "Does the Pope help these poor girls raise the babies they're forced to have?"

"Watch your tongue, young man," Liam said, rising from his seat. "Did anyone force these girls into bed with the fathers to begin with?"

"Yes," Brendan said evenly, "in some cases they *were* forced. I think Dr. Cassidy's doing a service to the community."

A vein in Liam's neck throbbed and he poked a finger in Brendan's face. "The man is a murderer."

"What?" Danny said.

"Any man who helps murder unborn children might just murder a priest as well."

"Now, come on, Liam," Tim Mahoney intervened. "Calm down."

Liam sat down and Danny began absently pacing from one end of the room to the other. "What about this Nigel Greene?" he asked Seamus as he set out another round of stouts. "And his wife Eleanor?"

"A strange couple," the publican said as he put a pint of stout on the bar.

"I find it odd," Tim Mahoney put in, "that Nigel went to the priest's last Mass, supposedly out of curiosity."

"The man's suspected of murder for going to Mass?" Liam asked.

"But he's not even Catholic," Danny said. Then he suddenly remembered something Nigel had said at Mrs. Slattery's table. "But you know," he added, "Nigel *did* know that December eighth was the Feast of the Immaculate Conception."

"There's something phony about him," said Brendan. "I don't trust 'im."

"Well, I could well imagine that wife of his killing

the husband to shut up his silly jokes," Liam offered, "but I certainly don't think either one of them would have killed Father O'Malley."

Danny was not so sure. Where was Eleanor while her husband was at Mass? It would take two people to drag the priest down to the basement. They had an opportunity, but no apparent motive.

Danny handed Seamus a twenty pound note for the round of stouts and studied the publican as he rang the till. Was Seamus involved? One thing was clear: he wanted to marry the Widow Conlon and Father O'Malley stood in his way. Seamus and Kathleen Conlon were both at Mass the morning the priest died, but they hadn't sat together. Were they still hiding their relationship from the villagers? Again, there were two of them to drag the priest to the basement, and Fidelma had said that perhaps the next priest to move into the parish would allow them to marry. Now Larkin seemed anxious for Danny to drop his investigation. To top it off, Seamus Larkin lived with his mother who, like James Roche, had diabetes. Larkin would also have access to a syringe.

"Where were you sitting at Mass?" Danny asked.

Larkin gave him a puzzled look. He picked up the pint of stout in front of him, wiped the bar with a rag, and set the jar back down. "What do you mean?"

Danny sipped his own pint. "Were you sitting up front, at the back of the church? Where?"

Larkin's eyes flicked to Liam Flynn then back to Danny. "About the middle I'd say. Why?"

"I'm just trying to get a sense of the layout of the church that day."

Larkin came from around the bar with a metal rod. Danny reared back, thinking he was going to hit him. But Larkin went over to the fireplace and poked the mound of turf with it.

"Can I ask you a personal question?" Danny said to the publican.

Larkin held up the metal rod and looked again at Danny as if he were ready to strike him. "Ask anything you want, though I won't be obliged to answer."

"Do you think you'll ever get married, Seamus?"

Larkin laughed nervously. "What sort of a question is that?"

"Just curious."

"What about you?" Larkin countered. "Haven't you been chasing Fidelma Muldoon long enough now?"

The color rose in Danny's face, "I haven't been chasing anyone."

"Oh, so she's the one chasing you?"

"What the hell are you talking about?"

"Right," said Larkin, brandishing the rod as he returned to his place behind the bar. "I don't know what the hell you're talking about, either."

Danny picked up his pint, and took a seat by the fire.

"I'm thinking," Brendan volunteered, "that Peggy Malloy has a few secrets."

"Yeah?" Danny asked.

"I'll bet a lot of things went on with her in Dublin that no one knows about."

Danny had to agree. There *was* something suspicious about Peggy Malloy. She had a questionable past, and seemed jumpy when Danny went to the house.

She apparently had had a key to the basement. What would be her motive? She was into tarot cards and crystals and she might be into devil worshipping as well. And she *did* have Pamergan in her medicine chest. That much was certain. If she knew her way around the Dublin drug scene, she'd have no trouble getting a syringe. But Danny couldn't really picture her killing her own son's pet cat. Unless the cat was completely unrelated to the murder of the priest.

"Do you think it's possible," Danny asked Brendan, "that Jeremy could be involved?"

"Jeremy Malloy?" Brendan exploded. "For God's sake, the lad's only ten years old."

"I know. But forget about that for a minute. Of everyone in the village, he had the best opportunity to give the sedative to the priest. In fact, of all the people in the church, Jeremy was the only one who was right next to Father O'Malley before, during, and after Mass."

"Oh, for the love of God," Liam Flynn sighed, "this is ridiculous. Next you'll have poor Desmond Conlon accused of it."

Desmond? Danny had not really considered him. Practically a part of the landscape, Desmond had the ability to be everywhere in the village without anyone paying much attention to him, and he *had* been at Mass that morning. He certainly had access to weed killer. Danny had seen him using the herbicide sprayer in Mrs. Slattery's garden. "Interesting thought," Danny said. "You know, he practically ran me over with a tractor."

"Oh, for the love of God," Flynn said again, into his jar of stout.

Danny sighed and rested his head on the heel of his hand as a wave of sadness passed over him. He felt guilty for suspecting everyone in the village. He'd even suspected Fidelma Muldoon. After all, Father O'Malley was the third priest to die while she was the house-keeper. Now, she up and leaves Ballycara with hardly any notice. Could Fidelma have put something in the priest's tea before Mass?

Maybe he should let it go. Maybe it *was* beyond his ken. But he couldn't stop turning the details over in his mind. And something else nagged at Danny: maybe Father O'Malley wasn't the good priest Danny thought he was. Sure, they had had fun times together, and he seemed to be a devout and devoted pastor. But there might have been a dark side Danny didn't know about, though he still didn't want to believe it.

Fifteen

Early the next morning, Danny went back to St. Bridget's to look around again. He retraced the steps Father O'Malley would have taken during Mass, and afterward in the sacristy. Then he gathered up the clothes that Father O'Malley had worn to church on the day of his murder, as well as the stole he had left behind on his dressing table. Danny placed them in a plastic bag, and caught a ride with Brendan Grady to Ennis where he turned the clothing over to Chief Superintendent Burke to have tested in the crime lab.

"O'Flaherty," Burke had begun gravely, "that was quite a blunder you made."

"I know. I'm sorry. I had no idea ..."

"Frankly, neither did I. Protected witnesses are well-guarded secrets."

"He was acting so suspiciously."

"Honest mistake, O'Flaherty. But I'll have to send a man out to Ballycara right away."

"I understand."

"We'll run a test on the garments, and I'll let you know what we find out. But from now on, you let me know before you start chasing anyone again."

"I will."

After meeting with the Chief Superintendent, Danny stopped at a pet shop in town.

"Do you have a black and white cat or kitten, by any chance?" he asked the clerk.

"I'm afraid the tabby is all we have right now as far as kittens. You did say you wanted a kitten?"

"That's right."

"Sure, the tabby is just eight weeks old. Is it a gift for someone?"

"Yeah, I'm buying it for a little boy who lost his cat."

"Then this one will be grand," said the clerk, placing the kitten in Danny's arms.

Since finding the Malloys' cat at the ring fort, Danny had toyed with the idea of buying Jeremy another one. He felt sorry for the little fellow. It was sad when Jeremy found out what had happened to his cat. Danny had gone back to the ring fort with a shoebox, put the cat's body in it, and brought it to the Malloys to bury. He wanted to do more.

He inspected the kitten as it tried to untangle its claws from the arm of his Aran sweater. He paid for the kitten, which the clerk put in a cardboard carrying case, and got a lift back to Ballycara with Brendan.

As they passed the Widow Conlon's place, Desmond had the hood of Mrs Slattery's car open and a rubber mat on the ground littered with tools.

"I hope he knows what he's doing," Danny said.

"Don't worry. He'll fix it," Brendan said, stopping in front of the Malloys' house.

Danny got out and slammed the door.

"I can wait if you want," Brendan offered through the window.

"That's okay. I'll walk back to Shannonside. But thanks for the lift."

"Not at all." Brendan was gone in a cloud of exhaust.

The sun shone brightly but the wind knifed through Danny's sweater as he walked up the driveway to the Malloys' house. He hid the kitten behind his back and knocked at the door.

Peggy Malloy opened it. "It's you," she said, eyes narrowed.

"Is Jeremy home?"

"What do you want with Jeremy this time?"

"I have a gift for him."

Just then the cat let out a high-pitched *meow*. Peggy smiled, invited Danny in, and called over her shoulder, "Jeremy! You've a visitor."

Danny reached into the cardboard box and held up the kitten by the fur on the back of its neck. When Jeremy came into the living room and saw the kitten, he dropped his book and raced toward Danny with outstretched hands.

"Is it for me?" asked Jeremy as he stroked and cuddled the cat.

"You bet it is, pal."

"Can I bring you something to drink, Mr. O'Flaherty?" asked the boy's mother.

"Nothing, thanks." Danny said, pointing to the box, "Shall we put this in your room?"

"I'll show you," said Jeremy, and Peggy nodded as Danny followed the boy into his room.

A clipping from *The Clare Champion* on the wall of Jeremy's room caught Danny's eye. It showed Father O'Malley flanked by two altar boys. One of them was Jeremy. Father O'Malley, in black, loomed over the children. The caption read: "Father Padraic O'Malley stands before the newly renovated church at Ballycara, County Clare." A brief article described the recent renovations of the church undertaken by Father O'Malley.

Danny set the box down in a corner of the room and watched Jeremy play with the kitten on his bed. After a while Danny asked, as gently as he could, "Jeremy, do you have any idea who might have killed your cat?"

Jeremy became suddenly somber. He shook his head.

"You know how we found it?"

Jeremy nodded.

The door to the boy's room stood open and Danny could feel Peggy Malloy's presence in the hallway. Difficult questions needed to be asked and Danny was determined to ask them. "You're sure, Jeremy, you have no idea who did it?"

The boy said nothing.

"Now Jeremy," Danny began. "You know, I think whoever hurt your cat might have also hurt Father O'Malley. What was your cat's name?"

"Tom."

Danny smiled. "When did you first discover Tom missing?"

"Just before you came over to see us last time. I called and called him but he never came."

"You kept him outside?"

"During the day."

"And you have no idea who might have done this?"

Jeremy didn't answer. He watched the kitten bliss-fully chewing on his shoelace.

Danny felt certain the boy was hiding something. He seemed scared. In fact, Danny had begun to feel that little Jeremy Malloy might hold the key not only to the death of his cat at the ring fort, but to the death of Father O'Malley as well.

Was Jeremy trying to protect his mother? She seemed suspicious and unhappy when Danny came around. "You're sure you don't know who hurt your cat?"

"Positive," the boy said.

Danny hesitated a moment. "Jeremy," he said gently, "I don't believe you."

"That's enough, now, do you hear!" The boy's mother came into the room. Her face was crimson as raw steak and a vein on her forehead pulsed. "What are you trying to do to my Jeremy? What do you mean you don't believe him?"

"It's all right, Mummy."

"It's not all right." She pointed a bright red finger-nail at Danny. "You come in here with your gifts like some big shot and then start tormenting my poor boy. He's done nothing; he knows nothing. Don't you have anything better to do with your time?"

"His cat was hung by the neck."

"I know that, the poor child. Can't you see he's upset enough?"

"And Father O'Malley was murdered."

"What do you want from us?" she shouted in exas-peration.

"I believe Jeremy knows something. I think he's too scared to tell."

"Of course he's scared," she let slip.

"What are you trying to hide?" Danny asked.

"We've nothing to hide."

"I think someone into occult stuff killed Jeremy's cat," said Danny.

"I don't know what you're talking about."

"Listen," Danny continued, "whoever killed Father O'Malley had a key to the basement. He or *she* opened the basement, forced Father O'Malley down there, shot him with herbicide, and came back up and locked the door afterwards, and you're the only other person in Ballycara who had a key to the basement."

Peggy Malloy glared at Danny as if she were ready to strike him. "I gave that key back!"

"You might have had it copied."

"We have nothing more to say to you. We've told you everything we know—which is nothing at all. Now, you may take your cat back with you and be gone."

"Mummy, please!" cried Jeremy, clutching the kitten as if it were a life raft. The boy trembled as he held on to the kitten and turned with wide eyes from Danny to his mother.

"Jeremy, I think you'd best give the man back the cat."

"But, Momma. Why can't I keep it?" The boy clutched the kitten so tightly Danny thought he might strangle it. Tears welled in his eyes and threatened to spill down his freckled cheeks. "Let me keep the kitten, Ma."

Peggy Malloy's eyes shifted back and forth from Jeremy to Danny. She reached out and took Jeremy into her arms and held him. "What do you know about the priest, child?"

"There was a man," he blurted suddenly, dropping the kitten, who scampered into a corner. Jeremy threw his arms around his mother.

"What was that?" asked Danny.

"There was a man who said something to me about Tom." The boy hugged his mother's waist.

"Jeremy, what in the world are you saying?" Peggy cried, holding her child at arm's length.

"He told me if I talked to anyone about the priest, he'd kill Tom."

"Now, Jeremy," his mother soothed, "you're imagining things."

He's trying to protect her, Danny thought, but he wanted an answer, too, so he didn't interrupt.

"I'm not imagining things. I saw him on my way home. When he passed beside me he said if I talked to anyone about Father O'Malley he'd kill Tom."

Danny looked down at Jeremy, who trembled as he struggled to hold back the tears.

"Who was he?" Danny asked. "What did he look like?"

"Desmond. He's the one who said he'd kill my Tom."

"Desmond?" Danny repeated.

"You've put ideas in his head," Peggy shouted at Danny. "That poor simpleton ..."

"Desmond Conlon?" Danny asked in amazement. "He's the one who said he'd kill your cat?"

"He is."

Danny let the knowledge sink in. "When did you last see Tom?"

"Monday noon," said Peggy.

"He was the one," Jeremy insisted, "who said he'd kill Tom if I talked about the priest."

"You're sure?"

"I am. Can I keep the kitten, Ma?" Jeremy asked again.

Danny held his breath, praying the woman would give in. The kitten licked Jeremy's finger.

"Oh, all right," she said. Then she turned to Danny. "I'm frightened. Why would Desmond do something like that?"

"I don't know," said Danny, "but I intend to find out."

Sixteen

Danny hiked briskly to the edge of Ballycara where the land rose to a small range of hills. The Widow Conlon lived with her son, Desmond, in a trim white stucco home with a slate roof. A stone fence enclosed the widow's tiny yard where Desmond repaired Mrs. Slattery's car.

"Is your mother home, Desmond?" Danny asked as he pushed open the wrought-iron gate and walked into the front yard.

Desmond did not look up from where he bent over the engine of the car. He held a socket wrench in his left hand and plunged his right hand deep into the guts of the engine, the tip of his tongue poking from a corner of his mouth. He jerked his head toward the front door.

Danny tried to imagine why Desmond would have hung Jeremy's cat. He couldn't picture Desmond doing it.

"Listen, Desmond," Danny began. "You know the day I saw you ride past the ring fort on your bicycle?"

Desmond dropped the wrench which clattered on the fender of the car.

Danny picked it up and handed it to him. "I was just wondering if you might know what happened to Jeremy Malloy's cat out there?"

Desmond stared at Danny as if the question had been asked in a foreign language. The blank look in Desmond's eyes made Danny uncomfortable. He cleared his throat and moved toward the front entrance. "Never mind," he mumbled.

Danny knocked at the door and Kathleen Conlon answered. She wore a beaded black gown of silk with a plunging V-neck bordered in gold thread. Danny's eyes followed her curves from the provocative leg-baring slit up the front of the dress to its sweeping fishtail train. She teetered on three-inch heels of suede leopard-print cocktail shoes.

Strands of gray weaved among her raven-colored hair and crow's-feet gathered at the corners of her eyes and mouth. Her cranberry lipstick looked as though it had been applied with a paintbrush.

Danny took a step back. "Mrs. Conlon?" he asked. He remembered the widow as a mousy spinster in a black shawl.

"Can I help you?"

When he found his voice he said, "My name is Danny O'Flaherty."

A look of alarm raced across the widow's features like a sudden wind that races across a quiet lake, rippling its surface. Her brow gathered in waves of wrinkles between her eyes. "I know who you are. I thought you lived up in Dublin."

"I do," said Danny. "But some of the folks here in

Ballycara have asked me to find out what I can about Father O'Malley's death. Do you mind if I come in?"

"I'm a bit busy," the widow said as she peered through the half-open door.

The sun had played hide and seek behind the clouds for most of the day and Danny shivered slightly. "This won't take a minute," he said.

Kathleen Conlon sighed. "Can you come back later?"

"As I said, I won't be a minute."

Her eyes flared, but she spoke calmly. "What is it you'd like to know?"

"I just have a few questions, if you don't mind."

The widow took a deep breath, let it out slowly, and opened the door. "Well, then, come in. And wipe your shoes." She turned, her bare back showing through the buckle-trimmed, ladder-backed halter of her gown.

"Thanks," he said, wiping his boots on the welcome mat before stepping into the cheerful kitchen.

"Cup of tea?"

"That would be too much trouble," Danny said hopefully.

"No trouble a-tall. I've the kettle warming already. Let's go into the parlor."

The house was tidy, had central heating, but a small turf fire burned in the tiny fireplace in the parlor. To Danny's surprise, Nigel Greene stood in the living room putting on his hat and coat.

"Do you know Danny O'Flaherty?" Kathleen Conlon asked.

Nigel nodded to Danny. "Yes, we know each other. I was just leaving."

"He was helping me fix the kitchen sink," Mrs. Conlon explained, smiling. "Weren't you ... Nigel?"

Danny wanted to ask her if she always wore an evening gown for the plumber, but thought it best to keep still.

Nigel Greene fumbled with the zipper on his jacket. His hands shook and he seemed to have trouble getting the zipper up.

After Nigel left, Danny sat in a wingback chair near the fire.

Mrs. Conlon returned with a Belleek teapot, two cups, and a half-empty bottle of Paddy Old Irish Whiskey. "Spice that tea up for you?" she asked, splashing a generous shot into her own cup.

"No, thanks." Danny studied the widow's outfit for a moment. "Am I keeping you from some ... engagement?" he asked.

"No," she said simply, as if a beaded silk gown and three-inch heels were standard attire for an afternoon at home.

"I guess you know we're still looking for the killer of Father O'Malley."

"Yes," she said. "What's Ballycara coming to at all? Rose Noonan killed two years ago and now Father O'Malley."

"It's a terrible tragedy."

"Sure, it's all the talk of the village now." She winked at Danny. "It'll give them something to talk about besides me."

Danny cleared his throat and began pleasantly. "I see Desmond's got Mrs. Slattery's car apart."

She smiled. "Yes. He'll have it all back together, I'm sure, and working better than it did."

Danny wasn't quite sure how to ask Mrs. Conlon about her son. What was he supposed to say, "By the way, has Desmond killed any cats lately?" So he went on to other matters. "I understand you were at Father O'Malley's last Mass."

Mrs. Conlon poured another shot into her tea, blew across it, and took a sip. "I was, yes."

"So you were there the day the priest died?"

"Yes." She watched Danny expectantly.

"Did you notice where Father O'Malley went after Mass?"

"Well, he went into the sacristy, as he usually does. But after that I didn't take any notice of where he went."

"How well did you know Father O'Malley?"

"As well as the next person, I suppose. He was our parish priest."

"Do you think he might have had any enemies in Ballycara?"

Mrs. Conlon shrieked with laugher. "Of course not. A parish priest always has people who like him and others who don't. But enemies?" She shook her head. "I don't think so."

"Is there anything you can tell me about the other people who were at Mass the morning he died?"

"What would you like to know?"

"Do you think any of them may have had something against Father O'Malley?"

Kathleen Conlon regarded Danny over her teacup. Her eyeballs bulged as she stared at him but there was something oddly out of focus about her gaze. "Mr. O'Flaherty, I'm not sure I understand your interest in all of this."

"Padraic O'Malley was my friend," Danny said. "Besides, Seamus and some of the others at the pub asked me to see what I could find out. I want to know what happened to him."

"We all do, Danny Boy. But that's the job of the Garda Siochana." She laughed. "You're just a blow-in yourself."

Danny studied the woman a moment. The wrinkles on Kathleen Conlon's cheeks and across her forehead seemed to fade and Danny could imagine a much younger, more beautiful Kathleen. "Mrs. Conlon," Danny asked, "did you like Father O'Malley?"

"We had our differences."

"What differences?"

"As you well know, I have been involved with Seamus Larkin for some years now since the death of my husband. There's no shame in that. My husband was killed on a building site in Birmingham, England, soon after we were married."

Danny slurped his tea and turned his gaze to the window. Outside, Nigel Greene was talking to Desmond. Probably telling him some dumb joke that Desmond would never understand.

"I have raised my son single-handedly," the woman went on. "That boy has never known his father."

Danny glanced again to the window. This time, Nigel and Desmond almost seemed to be arguing.

"When Father O'Malley came to this parish three years ago, Seamus and I approached the priest with our plans to marry. Seamus has been like a father to that boy and it's time we made it official." She reached down and slopped more whiskey into her tea.

Just then the door opened and Desmond stepped inside and slammed the door behind him. Wiping grease off his hands with a red rag, he walked briskly across the room, disappeared without a word into one of the bedrooms, and banged the door shut.

"Is he upset about something?" Danny asked.

"Desmond's a moody boy," she said.

Moody enough to hang a cat by the neck? He wondered. "Well, he's quite a mechanic," Danny said. "You must be proud of him."

Mrs. Conlon examined Danny for a moment as if trying to assess the tone of the comment. "Yes, I am."

"Was his father mechanically inclined?"

"Oh, yes. Mick Conlon was quite the mechanic."

"He must have been a big man. Desmond's built like a football player."

Mrs. Conlon seemed distracted. She stared into her teacup, then turned her eyes to Danny with the same unfocused gaze as before. "He was small, actually."

"How did you happen to meet him?"

"Who?"

Danny hesitated a beat. "Your husband, Mrs. Conlon. How did you happen to meet your husband?"

"Oh, him." Kathleen Conlon pulled her red lips into a sneer and sipped her tea. "I met Michael Conlon in the spring of 1972. Well, not met him, exactly. I'd known him most of my life. Like me, he had dreams of a future that did not include shoveling sheep shit in

Glenmore, Ireland, for the rest of his life. He was to get his leaving certificate that June." Widow Conlon brushed a loose hair away from her face. "He planned to go with two other fellows to London to find work in the building trade." She stared off as if lost in her reverie.

When she did not speak for a full minute, Danny quietly prompted her. "Mrs. Conlon."

Her attention snapped back to the present. "Can you imagine, Danny," she said, as if there had been no pause in her story, "how romantic a place like London sounded to a girl who had never left County Kerry? Sure, I thought it was the grandest thing one could imagine."

Danny had asked a simple question. He hadn't expected her life story. But she seemed to want to talk, so he let her. "What did your parents think of Michael?"

Kathleen Conlon fiddled with the gold embroidery on her gown. "My parents did not like Michael Conlon a-tall."

"Oh, really. Why not?"

"My people were a serious lot. Oh, yes, very serious. But Michael Conlon loved capers and stories. Besides that, he was a dreamer and a man who was not about to be confined by the expectations of small-town Ireland."

"Ambitious," Danny said. "Seems your parents would have liked him."

"Aye. But his main ambition was to get out of Ireland. Sure, they didn't want to see their little girl go away and never come back again."

"I can understand that."

"But Michael always talked about leaving. And the more he talked about leaving the more I thought that, sure, living in London would be a whole lot more exciting than Kerry."

"So you married him?" Danny said.

"Yes, then ran off to London. Later, Michael got a job on a building site: high rise tower blocks in Birmingham; government public housing. Desmond was born in May. When he was born we knew immediately that he wasn't quite right, but we loved him all the same. Less than a year later my husband made one false step on a scaffold, and was killed."

"In Birmingham?"

The widow hesitated. "That's right."

Danny watched her closely. "Then why did you come back to Ireland?"

"I had no choice. When my husband died there was no money, so I turned to my parents. My father gave me the money to come back and start my life over."

"I see."

"When I got back to Ireland, my father wanted me to give up my child. He wanted me to put Desmond up for adoption."

"Why?" Danny asked, astonished.

"Because he was afraid I couldn't give him the special care a child like Desmond needs."

"But you held onto him."

Widow Conlon said quietly, "Yes."

"Is your father still alive?"

"He lives in St. Mary's, a nursing home in Ennis." The left corner of her mouth twitched.

"I still don't understand why Father O'Malley wouldn't let you marry Seamus Larkin," said Danny.

Mrs. Conlon emitted a sound like a low growl.

"Excuse me?" Danny said.

The widow looked at him and flashed a brilliant smile. "I didn't say anything."

Danny looked at her, puzzled. "Do you think Seamus was angry enough about it to harm the priest?"

Just then Desmond came into the living room wearing a black flight jacket and carrying a tackle box in one hand and a fly rod in the other. His face was flushed as though he'd been crying.

"Goodbye, Mother," he said.

"Going fishing, Love?" She asked.

He stared at her.

"Be careful," she said.

"Goodbye, Mother," he repeated, and walked out the door.

Danny finished his tea. "I guess I've taken enough of your time, Mrs. Conlon. It was nice seeing you."

Kathleen Conlon stood up and walked Danny to the door. As they passed through the kitchen, Danny asked, "Mr. Greene get your plumbing fixed for you?"

The widow staggered slightly from the tea. "Yes. It was exceedingly kind of him."

Danny nodded. Desmond was not the only one in this family playing without a full deck. "Would you have any idea why Nigel Greene would have gone to see Father O'Malley?"

"What?"

Was she hard of hearing? "Fidelma tells me Nigel

spent an hour with Father O'Malley a couple days before he died."

Mrs. Conlon swayed slightly on her heels and for a second her eyes lit up like a jack-o'-lantern's, and Danny thought she might fall.

When he reached out to steady her she hissed, "Don't touch me." Then her features relaxed, she stood erect, and smiled brightly. "How in the world would *I* know why he went to see the priest?"

Danny regarded the widow warily and stepped backwards. "Just a thought." He put on his hat and opened the front door. "Thanks again." He stepped outside and heaved a sigh of relief. *What a nut!* "And thanks for the tea."

"No trouble a-tall."

Seventeen

Danny spent the rest of the day going over the crime scene with the detective that Chief Superintendent Burke had assigned to the case. They walked through the church as Detective Sargeant Devins took photographs. In the sacristy, the detective took measurements with a tape, and drew a rough sketch of the layout.

Two technicians from the crime lab took fingerprints from the door knobs and changing table, then they all went down into the basement where Danny pointed out where the body was found, its position, and answered dozens of questions.

After Detective Sargeant Devins and the techs packed up and left, Danny strolled in the direction of the pub. Just as he passed Larkin's Pub, Tim Mahoney drove up the street. Tim stopped the car and shouted out the window, "Danny. Desmond Conlon's gone missing."

"What? When?"

"I'm after talking to his mother. She's worried sick about him."

"What happened?"

"He went off fishing and hasn't come back. She's afraid something's wrong."

"I saw him leave with his fishing gear when I was at their house."

"Liam Flynn saw him pass up the way, toward Diarmuid and Grainne's Rock. I'm going up there now to look for him. Seamus and a couple other men are combing the area around the lighthouse at Loop Head, and Brendan set out with his father and two brothers to search the Shannon around Carrigaholt."

"Let's go," Danny said. He jumped into Tim's car and they took off down the street, past the Spar grocery store and the church, and turned onto the road leading to Carrigaholt. On both sides, freshly mowed hay lay in deep green pastures. To the left, the fields ran out to a line of cliffs that plunged into the Atlantic.

"I'm thinking we could walk out to the cliffs and see what we can find." Tim Mahoney grew grave. "He's been lost before. I'll bet he just forgot how to get home. You know how Desmond is."

"I don't think he's lost," said Danny, but he didn't elaborate. He was thinking about Desmond's behavior when he said "Goodbye" to his mother.

Tim parked the car on the road near Diarmuid and Grainne's Rock, then they climbed over a stone fence beside the road and headed across a hay field toward the sea cliffs. The wind from the Atlantic carried the aroma of salt and rotting seaweed mixed with the ubiquitous smell of turf smoke. A flock of gulls batted against the wind, then turned abruptly and were swept like a pile of leaves across the field.

When they reached the edge of the field the land plunged abruptly to the moiling sea below. To the east, the cliffs rose ever higher, while in the west they descended and eventually met the level ground in a wide expanse of beach a mile or two below Ballycara. Hundreds of feet below, the surf smashed against the rocks.

"You walk east," Danny said, "and I'll walk west. We'll meet back here."

"Right," Tim said, and set off walking along the cliffs.

Danny turned, scouring the edge of the sea for some sign of Desmond. He scanned the rocks below as he made his way along the cliffs and back in the direction of Ballycara. The sea crashed against the shoreline sending up spewing geysers of spray.

Danny searched for hours among the cliffs until it was too dark to see anymore. Discouraged, he retraced his steps. Tim Mahoney walked toward him with a flashlight in hand.

"Nothing?" Danny asked.

"Not a blessed thing."

They drove back to the pub where a noisy crowd gathered outside. They were soon joined by Seamus' group as well as Brendan and his father and brothers. "Nothing."

"Maybe he's been murdered, too," someone in the crowd shouted.

"Now, calm yourselves," Seamus Larkin intervened.

Mrs. Slattery comforted the Widow Conlon who sobbed uncontrollably.

"There's nothing more we can do tonight," Seamus said. "We'll all meet right here at daybreak tomorrow morning."

"Don't worry," Danny heard Mrs. Slattery say to the widow. "They'll find him."

Danny wasn't so sure.

Eighteen

"I'm afraid you're well past visiting hours."

Danny apologized, then pleaded to be allowed in. Finally, the nurse at St. Mary's Home for the Aged in Ennis relented, and pointed out Ciaran Early. Dressed in a faded yellow bathrobe, he sat in a recliner in the telly lounge holding a plastic cup and watching a late-night show from Dublin.

"Mr. Early," said Danny, who had borrowed Tim Mahoney's car and driven to Ennis after the search party broke up. "I'm a friend of your daughter, Kathleen."

The old man glanced up from the telly with a sour expression, then turned back to the news program. His cheeks were sunken and his eyes bulged from their bony sockets. He smacked his lips as if to rid them of a bitter aftertaste, and Danny saw he was toothless. He held his dentures in the plastic cup on his lap and stared at the telly.

"Are you feeling okay tonight?"

"Who wants to know?"

Danny faltered a moment. "As I said, I'm a friend of Kathleen's."

"Who are you?" the old man asked, squinting.

"Danny O'Flaherty."

"Means nothing to me."

"You don't know me. I'm American."

"That's obvious," said the old man, swirling his denture cup.

"I'm looking into the death of Padraic O'Malley."

"Who's Padraic O'Malley?"

"Father O'Malley, the parish priest of Ballycara. Surely, you know who I'm talking about."

"Dead you say? What happened to him?"

"No one knows for sure," said Danny. "All we know is that somebody shot him with a load of weed killer after Sunday morning Mass."

"Why come to me?"

"Your daughter, Kathleen—" Danny began.

"Listen here lad," the old man said, his voice rising, "I don't have a daughter."

"Of course you do."

Mr. Early glanced at Danny then focused his attention on the telly.

"Someone slipped a sedative to the priest, and when he conked out after Mass, that same person went in and dragged Father O'Malley into the basement where he finished the job."

"That so?"

Danny stepped between Ciaran Early and the television. "Is there anything at all you know that might be useful?"

"I have no idea what you're talking about," the old man answered. "Now, get out of my way."

Danny turned and pushed the off button on the T.V. "Someone killed a little boy's cat in the village."

"What has that to do with me?"

The problem was, Danny didn't know. "It might have been your grandson Desmond who did it, and now he's gone missing."

"Missing?"

"I think he's run away." Danny was stabbing in the dark. "Besides, I believe you're still angry about the way your daughter and Michael Conlon ran off to London years ago."

The old man's gaze flicked around the room maliciously. "I hated Conlon for what he did."

"Tell me about it."

"Michael Conlon nearly ruined my daughter's life. He disgraced our family. Everyone in the village back home knew Conlon got my Kathleen pregnant before they were married."

Danny sat down. So, Kathleen had already been pregnant when she got married. Then, she and Michael Conlon ran off to London. A detail she had failed to mention.

The old man stared at the dentures in his cup.

"What year did Conlon die?" Danny asked.

"Die?" The old man looked up. "Mick Conlon is alive."

Danny regarded Ciaran Early with horror. The old man was as crazy as his daughter. "Michael Conlon has been dead for twenty years."

Ciaran Early smiled. "Kathleen told you that, didn't she?"

"What are you talking about?"

"Mick Conlon is alive and well. Kathleen has been passing herself off as a widow all these years. She's always been a liar."

So, Danny thought, *maybe that's why Father O'Malley refused to let her marry.* If he knew Michael Conlon was still alive, officially, she was still married. "Why did she do that?"

"Because Mick Conlon turned out to be a drunken, abusive bum and she left him."

The widow Conlon was no stranger to booze herself, Danny thought.

"I helped her come back to Ireland. But she couldn't remarry. Divorce has been illegal here until just recently. Sure, there's a waiting list a mile long now for divorces in Ireland."

"You tried to force her to give up her child for adoption."

"Sure, I didn't think she'd be able to handle him." The old man tapped his forehead with a finger. "Not the full shilling."

Danny wasn't sure whether that meant Desmond or his mother. "And Michael Conlon never tried to see her, or Desmond?"

The old man turned away.

"Well, did he?"

When the old man spoke again, Danny could barely hear him. "Mick Conlon came here to see me."

"When?"

"The week before the priest died."

"So you did know about the priest's death."

"It's been on telly and in all the papers. I'm old, but I'm not senile."

"Did you know Father O'Malley?"

"Sure, I did. They all grew up together."

"What?"

"He was from Glenmore. Padraic O'Malley, Mick Conlon, and my daughter all grew up together."

Danny slapped his forehead with the palm of his hand. *Of course.* "What did Conlon want when he came here?"

"He was looking for Kathleen. He said he'd taken the pledge. He's off the drink now and lives with an English woman. He even passes himself off as English. Sure, he's been over there for twenty years, but he's no Englishman."

"Why did he come to see you?"

"He's in this Alcoholics Anonymous thing. Said he was working on his Eighth and Ninth Steps." The old man reached into his wallet and removed a laminated card with the Twelve Steps printed on it and handed it to Danny. "Step Eight: Made a list of all persons we had harmed, and became willing to make amends to them." Danny glanced at the old man and then back down at the card. "Step Nine: Made direct amends to such people wherever possible, except when to do so would injure them or others."

"Then why is he pretending to be someone else?"

"He said he didn't want to betray Kathleen. He knew she'd been passing herself off as a widow. He didn't want to hurt her or Desmond. He didn't want to give her secret away, but he wanted to see his son."

"Could Michael Conlon have had something to do with killing the priest?"

"Why would he?" asked Ciaran Early. "He said he wanted to see Kathleen to ask her for forgiveness, and he wanted to make amends to Desmond for the way he had neglected him."

"Do you have any idea where Desmond might be now?"

"I'm sorry. I don't know."

Nineteen

The next morning the search parties gathered again in front of Larkin's Pub. Danny and Tim teamed up and continued searching among the cliffs. Around noon, they heard a shout. Someone farther up the way called and waved his arms.

Danny looked at Tim in surprise. "Is that Desmond?"

"I think so."

Danny and Tim ran toward the man who waved and called out to them, but when they reached him, they saw it wasn't Desmond, but Brendan Grady pointing down the side of the cliffs. Soon, Brendan was joined by his father and brothers. "We started farther up the shore," Brendan explained, "and made our way down here. Look," and he pointed to the sea below.

A black jacket was wedged between the rocks and being jostled by the surf.

"Let's go down," Danny said.

"Sure, we'll break our necks," said Brendan, indicating the sharp slope of the cliff.

"Ah, we can make it," said Tim. "We used to climb all over these cliffs when we were lads."

All three of them picked their way carefully down the sheer rocky slope leading to the water's edge. Brendan led the way, followed by Tim, both carefully placing their feet on the rocks and hanging on as they lowered themselves. Danny came after, struggling for a foothold on the rocks, slippery with lichens and moss. With two hands raised above him gripping the ledge overhead, and his feet probing for a foothold, Danny looked over his shoulder at the furious ocean below. A wave of vertigo passed over him and he gasped. Sweat poured from his shaking hands as he struggled to keep his grip on the ledge above. Then his right foot found a hold and he lowered himself to a small ledge.

Afraid to look down again, Danny picked his way along the sheer cliff. He eased around an outcropping, again clinging to a crevice overhead, but his boots dangled in midair, unable to find solid footing. He kicked and struggled.

Danny could hear the ocean roar beneath him, and he intoned a silent prayer. His wrists ached from gripping the rocks, and he dug his fingernails into the unyielding stone. When his foot found a solid rock he lowered his weight onto it and released his hold on the crevice, breathing a sigh of relief.

Suddenly, the earth gave way beneath him, and an avalanche of rocks spilled out from under his boots. Danny reached for support and smashed his arm against a rock as he grasped desperately for a hold. For a moment he saw the sea rising up to him, and he cried out as he slid down the face of the cliff, twisting his ankle and scraping the skin off his elbow. "Shit!"

he screamed and suddenly landed on his side on a small outcropping ten feet below.

"You all right?" Tim shouted to him.

Terrified, Danny looked down at the violent sea below him, his heart drumming, and struggled to recover his breath while clinging tightly to a rock. He rubbed his arm where he had bruised it, then stood, searching for a toehold with his boot. He winced from the pain in his twisted ankle, and looked for a way to get down from the ledge. Once he steadied himself, he moved carefully down until he joined the others. Then they descended the side of the cliffs toward a tiny triangle of sand where the sea met the cliffs.

Standing knee-deep in water, they gasped when the waves retreated, revealing a shirtless man wedged into a crevice in the sheer face of the cliffs.

"Oh my God," Tim gasped, blessing himself.

The corpse had already begun to bloat and seabirds had picked on the flesh of its back.

"Poor Desmond," Brendan said wearily. "God rest his soul."

Danny shook his head sadly. The body lay face down in the shallow pool of water between the rocks. "Widow Conlon will take it hard."

"She will," said Tim.

"Let's get him out of there," Danny said, moving toward the body. "We'll lay him up on the rocks until we can find some way to get him back. God knows we can't carry him up the side of this cliff."

Danny, Tim, and Brendan grunted as they hauled the waterlogged corpse out of the crevice and dragged it to a small ledge above the water. When Danny rolled the corpse over on its back, Desmond Conlon stared up at them, his face still innocent even in death.

Danny had been wrong about Desmond. Maybe he knew too much and whoever *did* kill the priest shoved Desmond off the cliffs to shut him up. Danny glanced at Brendan Grady.

A man and his son who owned a *currach*, a small fishing boat, brought the body back to Ballycara. In the early evening when it had been deposited at the undertaker's in Carrigaholt, Danny, Tim, and Brendan waited with the undertaker for the Widow Conlon to arrive.

Danny brushed the dirt and pebbles he'd picked up on the cliffs off his sweater, and explained to the undertaker where they had found the body.

The undertaker reached into his jacket pocket and removed a damp photograph. "We found this in his pocket."

Danny bent closer to look at it. It was a copy of the same photo he had found in Father O'Malley's desk of the priest as a young man with his arms around a girl.

Brendan drew a deep breath and expelled it. "The poor boy was never right in the head, you know. Desmond went down there to fish and must have gotten caught by the tide."

"Why fish down there?" asked Tim. "Sure isn't the fishing just as good off Loop Head?"

The undertaker shook his head sadly. "You know Desmond. Sure, he wasn't the most logical thinker."

Brendan Grady was noticeably silent.

Tim had been staring at the photograph, then pointed to the girl in the picture. "Isn't that the Widow Conlon?"

Just then the widow entered the funeral parlor supported by Mrs. Slattery. Kathleen Conlon's head rested on Mrs. Slattery's shoulder and the widow wept quietly.

The undertaker disappeared inside and returned momentarily pushing a cart covered by a white sheet.

"No!" Kathleen cried.

"You have to," said Mrs. Slattery. "It's for your own good as well."

When the undertaker pulled back the sheet, Kathleen Conlon howled with grief, broke free of Mrs. Slattery, and fell across the corpse. "Desmond, oh my poor Desmond," she cried, her whole body shaking with anguish. She sobbed hysterically and embraced her dead son. "Desmond, oh God please, Desmond!"

Mrs. Slattery tried to restrain her, but the widow lashed out, choking with heartache. "Desmond!"

Danny bent his head and blessed himself, then turned and walked out of the funeral home, while the mournful keening of Kathleen Conlon echoed in his head.

Twenty

Later that night at Shannonside, Mrs. Slattery said, "You've a visitor."

Fidelma Muldoon stepped out of the kitchen into the parlor.

"Fidelma!" Danny exclaimed.

She ran across the room and threw herself into his arms.

"What are you doing here?" he asked.

"I'm back for a visit."

"But you've only been gone a few days."

"I've missed you," she said, then added hastily, "Mrs. Slattery just told me about Desmond."

"And I suppose you've heard Roche is not our man."

"I did," said Fidelma. "I'm sorry. Have you learned anything since I've been gone?"

"A lot," Danny said.

They moved to the sofa in the living room and Danny caught her up on events of the last couple of days, including finding Desmond's body.

"Do you think someone might have pushed him?"

"I don't know."

"Maybe Desmond had something to do with Father O'Malley's murder."

"Maybe. But then a lot of other people could have, too," he said. "Do you have any idea why Father O'Malley would not marry Widow Conlon and Seamus Larkin?"

"No."

Danny hesitated a moment, then softly, so Mrs. Slattery wouldn't hear, "Because the widow isn't really a widow."

"What do you mean?"

"She's still married."

"But Michael Conlon died over twenty years ago."

"How do you know?"

"Sure, that's what Widow Conlon said."

"I know."

"She lied?"

"Her father told me that Conlon is still alive." Danny lowered his voice. "Fidelma, that woman lives in a dream world. You should have seen the way she was dressed when I went over there. Like she was going to a celebrity ball."

"I'll admit she's a bit eccentric."

"A bit eccentric? She's a nut case!"

"But why? Why did she lie about her husband?"

"Because he was an alcoholic and abused her. But now he's reformed and supposedly he came back to see her and make amends. But I can't help thinking he had something to do with Father O'Malley's death. I intend to ask her about that."

"Not now, Danny. Not with poor Desmond just dying."

Danny turned to make sure Mrs. Slattery was out of earshot. "She was pregnant with Desmond when she ran off to London all those years ago."

Fidelma looked at him angrily. "What has any of that to do with Father O'Malley?"

"I don't know, yet."

"Well, I'm sure the Widow Conlon has been through a lot. But now with Desmond gone I don't see what prying into her past is doing to solve anything."

Mrs. Slattery walked into the room. "You've a phone call, Danny."

It was Chief Superintendent Burke. Danny spoke to the garda for a few minutes, then hung up and said to Fidelma, "I've got news!"

"What?"

"The crime lab came up with traces of the sedative in the cruet of wine."

"So?"

"I've been thinking all along that someone slipped the sedative to Father O'Malley before Mass. But the cruets are set up in the aisle during Mass."

"You mean someone could have put something in the wine during Mass?"

"Exactly. I should have thought of that before. Even Dr. Cassidy said that if the sedative was taken before Mass, Father would have passed out during the Mass itself." Danny took a breath. "I've got a plan."

"Danny, please. No more of your capers."

"This is no caper," Danny said hotly. "I want to set a trap for the murderer. We'll start at the pub. Will you come with me?"

***

A half hour later, Danny and Fidelma walked into Larkin's Pub, strode up to the bar, and ordered two Harps.

Seamus Larkin leaned across the bar and said to Danny, "I heard they found a photograph of Father O'Malley in Desmond's pocket."

"Yes," Danny said.

"You don't think Desmond murdered the priest, do you?"

"I don't know. I think we need to search the area around the cliffs to see if there is anything besides the photograph that might link Desmond to the death of Father O'Malley."

"What does the photograph prove?" Larkin asked.

Danny sat back and lifted his pint. "The photograph proves nothing except that Father O'Malley and Kathleen Conlon grew up together in Glenmore. Did she ever mention that to you, Seamus?"

"Kathleen never talks about her past. At least not to me."

"Why?" Fidelma asked. "Why would Desmond kill Father O'Malley?"

"I don't believe he did," said Larkin. "Desmond's a gentle soul."

Danny said nothing. He had not told Fidelma, nor anyone else, that Desmond had threatened to kill Jeremy's cat. Besides, this so-called gentle soul practically ran him over with a tractor. Danny slurped from his pint and then cleared his throat. "Whoever did kill Father O'Malley," he said, "took the priest's keys from the loop on his belt. It's possible that he, or she, still has a key."

"Peggy Malloy had a key at one time," Fidelma reminded him.

Danny said, loud enough so that everyone in the pub could hear, "There's still one piece of evidence that no one knows about yet."

"What's that?" Liam Flynn asked with obvious curiosity.

Danny hesitated, trying to think of what to say next. "Down in the basement. Whoever killed Father O'Malley left something behind."

"Really?" Tim Mahoney seemed suddenly interested, too.

"Yeah. The detective missed something when we went over the crime scene."

"What are you talking about?" Seamus asked as he came from around the bar carrying a shot of Paddy Old Irish Whiskey for himself and pulled a chair up to the turf fire.

Danny had the full attention now of Liam, Seamus, Brendan, Tim, and Fidelma. "I'm not at liberty to say. But there was something left in the basement that is sure to incriminate the person who killed Father O'Malley. In fact, I'd go as far as to say that it positively identifies the killer."

"But don't you think Desmond did it?" Brendan asked, swallowing hard.

"No," Danny said, "I don't."

"Do you think whoever killed Father O'Malley killed Desmond as well?"

"Maybe."

"Why didn't you mention this basement thing before?" Brendan asked.

"I forgot about this one bit of evidence until now."

"You forgot?" said Larkin.

Danny stared into his pint, swirled it, took a gulp, and set it back down before him. "Let's just say I didn't fully realize the significance of it until now."

"Well, tell us, lad," Liam Flynn urged, fiddling nervously with his pipe.

"I can't," Danny said, standing up. "We really have to go."

The last thing Danny heard as the door shut behind them was Seamus Larkin muttering, "Bunch o' cod."

That evening at Shannonside, Mrs. Slattery set two fresh pots of tea, a plate of soda bread, and thick slices of Limerick ham on the dining room table.

Nigel and Eleanor Greene emerged from their room, suitcases in hand.

"The Greenes are leaving on the evening ferry from Rosslare," Mrs. Slattery said to Danny and Fidelma.

"Sure, I hope you've enjoyed your time here," Fidelma said, smiling.

Danny watched the couple's every move.

"It's been lovely," Eleanor said.

"Do you know how many Irishmen it takes to change a lightbulb?" Nigel began.

"Nigel," his wife hissed.

"Six," said Nigel. "One to hold the new bulb in the socket and five to get drunk until the room spins around."

Eleanor laughed nervously and said, "Mrs. Slattery, we've had a very restful vacation, despite the unfortunate death of your clergyman and that poor young man, Desmond."

Danny stared at Nigel. Something about his accent and his false cheer still bothered Danny. "I don't think you need to worry about that anymore," he said. "The murderer of Father O'Malley will soon be in custody."

"Oh, really?" Mrs. Slattery asked.

"When the guards find what was left behind in the basement, we'll know exactly who killed Father O'Malley."

Mrs. Slattery looked confused. "What's this about the basement?"

Danny buttered a piece of soda bread. "Whoever killed Father O'Malley left something in the basement that points the finger right at the killer."

"Why didn't you report it?" Nigel asked. His Adam's apple bobbed once, and he chewed on his lower lip.

"Well, to tell the truth, I didn't realize the significance of it right away."

"Tell us, so," Mrs. Slattery said eagerly.

Danny held his hands above his head. "I'm out of it now. I'll do what I should have done all along."

"Leave it to the Garda Siochana," Fidelma put in. "That's right."

"I'm sure they've the situation much in hand," said Mrs. Slattery as she spread her napkin on her lap.

"Well," Nigel said, gathering up their bags. "If we're going to catch the ferry in Rosslare, we'd better move along."

After dinner, Danny said to Fidelma, "Would you care to walk with me?"

"Sure," she responded, "'tis a lovely evening," and she offered her arm.

The failing light softly caressed the village as they sauntered in the direction of the Cobbler's Rock.

As they passed the Malloys' house Danny said, "I want to drop a few more pieces of cheese here at the Malloys."

"What are you talking about?"

"The trap I'm setting to catch a rat."

Jeremy Malloy answered Danny's knock and he turned and called over his shoulder. "Ma. It's Danny."

Peggy Malloy came to the door looking haggard. "What now?"

"I just want to say goodbye. I won't be bothering you anymore. I'll be leaving for Dublin soon."

Jeremy's little face fell. "I'll miss you, sure."

"I'll miss you, too, guy," Danny said. He reached out and put his hand on Jeremy's head.

"And we still don't know who killed Father O'Malley," Peggy said lightly.

"Oh, I think we'll know soon enough."

She raised her eyebrows. "We will?"

"Yeah," Danny said. "The killer left something behind in the basement that positively identifies who did it."

"What is it?" Peggy gasped.

"Something I saw down there the day we found Father O'Malley."

"You mean," she began, nervously rubbing her earlobe with her thumb and forefinger, "we'll know exactly who killed him?"

"Positively."

"But what is it?"

"I can't really say. It's up to the Garda Siochana now."

Danny held his hand out and Jeremy shook it. "I'll be seeing you, Jeremy. Take care of that cat."

"I will," Jeremy said with a catch in his voice.

"What did you name him?" Danny asked. "It's a male, isn't it?"

Color rose in the little boy's face and he looked away.

Peggy put her arm around Jeremy. "He calls him Danny Boy," she said.

"Well," Danny began, and now there was a lump in *his* throat. "I guess I've made enough of a mess here in Ballycara. Time to get back to Dublin." Danny chuckled. "It's always a mess there."

"You've done the best you can," said Peggy. "I'm sure the guards will catch the killer."

"Yeah," Danny said. She was a bad liar. "They'll take care of it."

"Why don't we drop over to Mrs. Conlon's and extend our condolences," Fidelma said. "See if there's anything we can do to help."

On the way to Kathleen Conlon's house, Danny breathed in the fresh smells of the countryside, the crisp air, the sound of the shrieking gulls. He was confident that Father O'Malley's murderer would soon be caught. He remembered that since moving to Ireland from New York, things he had hardly noticed before—the veins of a leaf, the sparkle of sunshine on grass, the smell of the air—had given him a new and intimate pleasure.

After a while Danny said, "There's something still bothering me about that Nigel Greene."

"Oh, he's not a bad sort," said Fidelma. "He just needs a new set of jokes."

"Do you know what *pisoig* means?" Danny asked.

"It means an old folk story or superstition. Why do you ask?"

"Is that a word an ordinary Englishman would know?"

"Not unless he's studied Irish. Why?"

"Nigel Greene used that word once at Mrs. Slattery's table."

"Did he, now?"

At Kathleen Conlon's house, Danny and Fidelma sat in front of the fire. This time Mrs. Conlon was dressed in a conservative blue cardigan and matching pants. Danny could hardly believe it was the same woman he had visited before. She stared listlessly as she handed them each a cup of tea. This time she did not offer whiskey. The blank look in her eyes, the listless stare, gave Danny the impression of a woman in shock.

"Kathleen," Fidelma began as Mrs. Conlon sat down with her own tea, "you know if there's anything we can do, don't hesitate to ask."

Kathleen Conlon, who had been silent up to this point, cried out piercingly, then pressed a crumpled tissue against her mouth and wept. "Poor Desmond," she murmured over and over again.

Fidelma patted her shoulder as Kathleen broke down again, her whole body trembling as she sobbed.

After a few minutes, she got herself under control, and asked between whimpers, "What about Father O'Malley?"

"Kelley is coming back from vacation tomorrow. He can handle it," Danny said.

"As it should be," Kathleen whispered. She stared as if in a trance at a lamp across the room.

Danny cleared his throat. "There is one piece of evidence left in the basement that I think will easily pinpoint the killer."

Mrs. Conlon looked up at him, wide-eyed. She dabbed at her eyes with the tissue balled up in her fist. "Really?"

"Not even Kelley could miss it," Danny quipped. "I'll leave it to him. But there is still one thing I'd like to know from you, Mrs. Conlon."

"What's that?" she asked.

Danny looked at her as if steadying his nerves. "Why wouldn't Father O'Malley marry you and Seamus?"

"Danny!" Fidelma gasped.

"I told you," said Mrs. Conlon without missing a beat. "I don't know why he wouldn't."

Danny felt sorry for Kathleen Conlon, but he plunged ahead. "You're not a widow, are you?"

"What?"

"I said, you're not a widow."

"I am."

"Not if Michael Conlon is still alive."

Mrs. Conlon put her head down and when she looked back up her eyes blazed with fury. "Mick Conlon was a drunken bum. Was I to stay with him just because there was no divorce in Ireland?" Her voice trembled. "I left him—and I've never regretted it for a moment."

"And now he's come back to ask for your forgiveness."

"I don't know what you're talking about," said Mrs. Conlon.

Fidelma put her arm around Kathleen Conlon and glared at Danny.

"He came back," Danny went on, "to make amends for the trouble he gave you, and to ask Desmond to forgive him for not being a better father."

Mrs. Conlon put her head in her hands and quietly wept, then pulled a tissue from her pocket and blew her nose.

"He came here masquerading as an Englishman. He was here the other day."

"I have no idea what you're saying."

"I'm talking about Nigel Greene."

"What did you say?" Fidelma asked, looking confused.

"Nigel Greene knew the date of the Feast of the Immaculate Conception because he is a Roman Catholic, like everyone else in Glenmore. Right, Mrs. Conlon?"

She turned her face away.

"Nigel Greene can mimick perfectly the accent of an Irish farmer in his jokes because he grew up among Irish farmers. Nigel Greene works in the building trades in Birmingham, just as you said your husband did. And Nigel Greene knows the meaning of the Irish word *pisoig* because he himself is an Irishman."

"This is ridiculous," said Kathleen.

"Nigel Greene was at your house the day I was there because he is your husband, isn't he? Nigel Greene is really Michael Conlon."

"He's not my husband as far as I'm concerned," Kathleen said quietly. "He's asked for my forgiveness, but I won't give it. Now he can go back to England. Just because he's sober now doesn't undo everything he did to Desmond and me." Kathleen Conlon stood up wearily. "Now, please go. I really wish to be alone."

"Will you be all right?" Fidelma asked.

Mrs. Conlon nodded.

Outside, Fidelma turned on Danny. "How could

you hound that poor woman like that?" she hissed. "She's in mourning."

"I know. And I'm sorry about Desmond. But we've got to find out what happened to Father O'Malley."

"You said Kelley's coming back tomorrow."

"That's right."

"You think this Nigel Greene killed Father, don't you?" Fidelma said.

"Whoever killed Father O'Malley took his keys off his belt and probably still has them," said Danny, "including the key to the church basement."

"But who?"

"Well, if our plan works, we'll soon know, won't we?"

Twenty-One

Darkness had fallen over Ballycara as Danny said goodnight to Fidelma and made his way toward St. Bridget's. He opened the creaking doors of the church and slipped inside out of the chilly night air. Votive lights burned under the statue of the Blessed Virgin.

Danny dipped his fingers in the font of holy water, blessed himself and walked up the aisle, past the Stations of the Cross. He paused in front of the twelfth station—Jesus Dies on the Cross. Danny shivered slightly, feeling a sudden chill in the gloomy interior of the church, and continued toward the sanctuary.

There was a small table halfway to the altar, on the left side of the aisle, where the offertory gifts were placed during Mass. Danny had put too much emphasis on finding out who may have had access to the wine *before* Mass. Now he saw clearly that whoever sat beside the table had dropped the sedative into the wine during Mass. He hesitated for a moment beside the table, then walked toward the sanctuary.

Standing before the altar, Danny tried to picture Father O'Malley alive, to remember his voice, his laugh, the hours of lively conversation they had enjoyed. He also tried to imagine how anyone could have taken the priest's life, although now he was sure he knew who had.

He intoned a silent prayer for the priest's soul, and for Desmond Conlon's, and once again tried to compose a proper way to ask for assistance in his search.

When he had first come to Ballycara, Danny had been reluctant to ask for help in finding Father O'Malley. Maybe it was excessive pride. But tonight he needed strength—perhaps a miracle—to catch the priest's killer. Danny glanced up briefly at the statue of St. Joseph to the right of the altar, then passed through the sacristy door.

Something eerie about the darkened room at this time of night quickened Danny's pulse as he looked around the interior. Again, he imagined Father O'Malley's last Mass and he prayed that his friend had not suffered before he died.

Danny walked to the back of the sacristy and inspected the door leading to the cellar. It remained locked with the same lock they had opened the day he and Fidelma had found the priest's body; Danny still had *that* key in his pocket.

Father O'Malley's killer had the other.

Looking for a good place to hide, Danny spotted the priest's wardrobe. He opened it and shoved aside the cassocks and altar clothing hanging inside.

Danny spent a cold, uncomfortable night crouched in the wardrobe, through which he had a partial view of the hatch into the basement. He dozed throughout the night, his legs aching from the cramped position.

By midnight, Danny's knees were so cramped from sitting in the priest's wardrobe that his legs fell asleep. He kneaded his calves, trying to rub the ache from them, then drifted off to sleep. At one point he thought he heard someone open the door of the sacristy, but it was merely the wind.

Later, he was jolted awake by a banging sound. He touched a button on the side of his watch that lit up its face: four AM. Danny twisted around and put his left eye to the crack in the wardrobe. He heard another sound near the basement door. He strained to see through the crack, and could barely make out a human shape moving toward the hatch.

Danny held his breath, straining for a better view. He heard the metallic ping of something hitting the floor and someone cursed softly in the darkness. Then he heard the click of the padlock opening, the thump of the lock dropping on the floor, and the squeal of the door's hinges as it opened.

He smiled with satisfaction. The rat was looking for the cheese.

He stayed crouched in the wardrobe listening to the other person going down the stairs. He waited until whoever went into the basement would be well clear of the stairs, then eased himself out of the wardrobe and stretched his aching legs. A sharp pain speared the middle of his back and he stretched and bent to work it out.

Danny moved to the door of the basement. The rat, indeed, had entered the trap. The open padlock lay beside the cellar door, although the door itself had been closed.

Danny crept toward the basement door and seized the padlock. Below he heard someone moving around in the cellar. The movement stopped, as if whoever was down there had heard Danny moving above and paused to listen. Then he heard footsteps again and something being shoved aside downstairs.

Danny eased the padlock through the hasp on the basement door and clicked the trap shut.

A dozen people gathered for Sunday Mass at St. Bridget's that morning. The new priest, Father John Murphy, genuflected before the altar, flanked by two altar boys, Jeremy Malloy and Marty Kelley. The priest turned and faced the congregation. "May the fellowship of the Holy Spirit be with you all."

"And also with you," the congregation answered.

"The intention of today's Mass," said Father Murphy, "is for the repose of the souls of Father Padraic O'Malley and Desmond Conlon."

Danny O'Flaherty lowered his head, blessed himself, and intoned a silent prayer. What a crazy week it had been. But if he was right this time, the murderer of Father O'Malley was trapped at this moment in the basement of the church. If he was wrong ... Danny didn't want to think about that.

"To prepare ourselves to celebrate the sacred mysteries, let us call to mind our sins."

Well, Danny thought, they were probably too numerous to recall in one sitting. He owed an apology to Fidelma Muldoon for losing his temper, and he certainly owed an apology to Peggy Malloy.

Halfway through Mass, Danny heard a muffled shout from the basement of the church. Father Murphy glanced back toward the sacristy as if he, too, had heard something, and then he looked down at the floor.

Just as the priest concluded Mass, another shout rose from the basement. This time Danny stood and walked to where Garda Kelley, looking sunburned and rested from his vacation, knelt near the front of the church.

"Welcome back," said Danny.

"What's going on, O'Flaherty?" Kelley whispered. Obviously, he too had heard the noises.

"I set out some bait for Father O'Malley's killer. Shall we go see what's in the trap?"

"What are you talking about, O'Flaherty?"

"Let me out!" someone shouted and when a loud bang rose from the floor of the church, several people began whispering.

"The Mass is ended," said Father Murphy as he looked around, bewildered. "Go in peace to love and serve the Lord."

As the priest exited through the front of the church, led by Jeremy Malloy carrying the banner of the Sacred Heart of Jesus, and Marty Kelley carrying the cross, another shout rose from the basement. "Let me out of here!"

"What in the name of God is that?" said Mrs. Slattery loud enough so that several people responded.

"I heard it, too," Liam Flynn said.

"Is this another one of your capers, O'Flaherty?" asked Garda Kelley.

"You might say so. Shall we have a look?"

A crowd gathered beside Danny and Garda Kelley as they walked into the sacristy. Father Murphy had taken off his vestments and pointed toward the cellar door. "There's someone down there," he said.

"I know," Danny answered. "Only one other person has a key to this basement. Whoever killed Father O'Malley took the priest's keys from his belt the morning of the murder. When I put out the word that there was incriminating evidence left at the crime scene, that same person used the priest's keys to go back down into the basement to find out what was left behind."

"There was nothing down there," said Kelley defensively.

"Of course there wasn't. But the murderer didn't know that."

"You mean he's down there now?" asked Father Murphy.

"I'm willing to bet that whoever's in the basement killed Father O'Malley." Danny looked around at the crowd gathered in the sacristy. He already knew who they would find. He handed his key to Garda Kelley. "I guess it's time to let the Garda Siochana take over."

Twenty-Two

Kelley snatched the key from Danny's hand, moved toward the basement door, inserted the key in the padlock, and unlocked it. The hatch of the basement burst open, knocking Kelley on his rump.

Kathleen Conlon climbed out.

Her dishevelled hair hung to her shoulders and she wore torn jeans and a dingy woolen sweater. Her eyes shone with the crazed glow of a cornered animal.

"You?" Mrs. Slattery said, her mouth falling open. "What in God's name have you done?"

The people from Mass crowded the sacristy door, anxious to see what was going on.

Kelley got up from the floor, brushed off the backside of his pants, and squared his shoulders while the parishioners gathered around Kathleen Conlon in an angry mob. For a moment Danny feared they might tear her apart.

"I don't understand," said Mrs. Slattery. "What in the world did you have against Father O'Malley?"

Danny watched her carefully.

"Tell us," Kelley prompted.

Kathleen Conlon looked from face to face as if trying to settle on a sympathetic ear. Sweat had broken out on her upper lip and she grimaced as if in pain. "I haven't done anything. It's all your fault," she screamed at Danny.

"What were you doing down there?" Kelley asked.

"This American," she said, pointing at Danny, "he's crazy. He lured me down here and trapped me in the basement. I've been locked in there all night."

"Why did you go down there?" asked Kelley.

"I want him arrested!"

Just then, Nigel and Eleanor Greene came into the sacristy.

"You're back," Danny murmured.

"Tell them, Kathleen," Nigel said. Although he had apparently acquired some English pronunciations from his many years in Britain, he had dropped the heavy English voice he had been using and his own Kerry brogue came through. "You have to tell them the truth now, Kathleen."

"What's this about?" asked Kelley.

"My name's not Nigel Greene. I'm Kathleen's husband, Michael Conlon."

The crowd of people at the door of the sacristy struggled to get a better look.

Kelley looked at him, mouth agape. "I thought your husband was dead," he said to Kathleen.

"Let me explain," she whispered. "This is all a mistake."

"Start explaining," said Kelley.

"You don't know what it's like," she said meekly, "when someone leaves you with a baby on the way."

"What's she talking about?" Peggy Malloy asked as she held Jeremy in a protective embrace.

"He left me," she said to Peggy as if finally finding a sympathetic ear.

Danny watched Kathleen. Although he shuddered from the thought of what she had done, he almost felt sorry for her.

"You left her?" Kelley asked Nigel.

"No. You see, Kathleen and I, and Father O'Malley," Nigel began, "all grew up in the same town, Glenmore in County Kerry."

Kathleen broke in. "Padraic O'Malley was the eldest son in his family and destined for the seminary. It was the oldest boy's obligation, at least in that family, to become a priest."

Daylight illuminated the interior of the sacristy, and Kathleen stared for a moment at the stained glass window above her with its scene of the scourging—Christ being whipped by the Roman soldiers.

"That was in the spring of nineteen seventy-two." She wrinkled her forehead as if from the effort it took to bring back those long passed years. "I'd known Padraic O'Malley most of my life. We were both finishing school. But there were few prospects for women in those days. It may not be much different now. You might marry the farmer next door if he were the eldest and coming into the farm. And if you had no prospects for marrying a farmer you might emigrate like my two brothers did."

The people in the sacristy watched her curiously.

She took a tissue from her pocket and dabbed at her eyes. "I loved him. He was sensitive, well-mannered, polite, and deeply religious. He had dreams of a wife and family, but his parents wanted him to become a priest."

"Did he ever talk to you about going into the seminary?" Danny asked gently.

"He didn't want to go. His parents were the ones who wanted him to be a priest." She looked from face to face with a pleading expression. "He wanted to marry me. He promised me he would." She closed her eyes a moment then opened them. "He loved me."

"So why did you marry this man?" Kelley asked, pointing to Nigel Greene.

She ignored Kelley and continued her story. "Padraic's parents tried to keep me away from their son. But every night we'd meet at an abandoned quarry." Kathleen's eyes sparkled from the memory. "We laughed and talked and dreamed of when we'd be man and wife; when we'd have a family."

Kathleen paused and folded her hands as if in prayer. "Then something happened." Her eyes moved around the sacristy, then finally settled on Danny's face. "I got pregnant."

Danny nodded. For an unmarried woman to get pregnant in rural Ireland in those days was serious trouble.

"Not by Michael Conlon?" Kelley asked.

Kathleen turned to Nigel. "I hardly knew him. He was the town fool. No, I was pregnant by Padraic O'Malley. I was going to have his baby."

The crowd in the sacristy began to whisper all at once.

"I don't believe this," shouted Seamus Larkin.

"What happened then?" Kelley removed his notebook from his suit pocket and scribbled in it.

Kathleen lowered her head, and when she raised it her eyes filled with tears. "When Padraic O'Malley found out I was pregnant"—her voice changed pitch and she cried out—"he left me! He ran away, and I hated him for doing that to me and our child."

"His parents forced him to join the seminary," Danny said.

"I don't care what his parents did. He abandoned me and my child!"

"Go on," Kelley said.

"When I realized I was pregnant and that Padraic had left me ..." Mrs Conlon looked down at her hands, inspecting the cuticle on her left thumb, then up to Nigel Greene.

The crowd in the sacristy waited breathlessly.

When she spoke at last her voice was a whisper. "You have to understand, it would have ruined my life. I had to find a husband and a father for my baby. They might have sent me to a mother-baby home. That's what they did in those days. They sent unwed mothers to a home where they had their babies. Then they took the baby away from you. I couldn't let that happen."

She motioned with her chin in Nigel's direction. "So, I seduced this man down by the old quarry. When I started to show, I told my parents it was his baby."

"Can you imagine?" Mrs. Slattery whispered, scandalized. "And they believed you?"

"Yes, they believed me. And my father forced this man to marry me."

"I believed you, too," Nigel broke in. "I loved you,

Kathleen. Your father and I both believed I was the father of the child," Nigel added. "I believed it all these years, too."

"What did you two do?" Kelley asked them.

"The day after we married we left for London," said Nigel. "I got a job on a building site in Birmingham. There were complications with the pregnancy. At first the doctors didn't think the baby would make it a-tall."

Kathleen cut him off. "The more problems I had in the pregnancy, the more I hated what Padraic O'Malley had done to me." Her eyes blazed with anger, then suddenly the fire in them went out and she smiled. "Desmond was born in May. I had a fever during labor and the doctors were afraid my baby would die. But he didn't. He was a beautiful baby. At first I thought he would be fine."

Nigel cut in, "But we soon realized little Desmond was not normal."

"You weren't normal, either," she yelled at Nigel.

"I wasn't, Kathleen," he said, hanging his head. "When Desmond turned out the way he did, it drove me to drink. I blamed myself." He shook his head. "And now, to find out he was never really my son—" Nigel took a deep breath as if gathering his strength. "About a year after Desmond was born, I was nearly killed. I'd been drinking on the job, and fell off a scaffold."

Danny added, "And Kathleen Conlon just embellished the story of the accident a bit and made it sound like you were killed on the building site. She just pretended you were dead and left you."

"That's right," Kathleen said. "I never loved him.

I went back to Ireland. As far as I was concerned, he *was* dead. I still thought maybe I could get back with Padraic. Besides, I had no money. My father gave me the money to come back and start my life over in Ireland." Mrs. Conlon's mouth tightened into a grimace. "When I got back to Ireland my father wanted me to give up my child. He tried to force me to put Desmond up for adoption. He said I had no other choice, that I couldn't provide for myself, let alone a child. Especially one with Desmond's problems."

"But you kept your baby," Danny said, trying to reveal some compassion inside Father O'Malley's murderer. "You raised him yourself."

Mrs. Conlon began to cry quietly. "Yes. But I still wanted Padraic. I thought when he saw his child he'd come back to me. But by then he had already been accepted into the seminary in Maynooth." She stopped sniffling and her lips curled into a sneer. "Oh, yes! He was on his way to becoming a fine Catholic priest. And I was raising his child alone."

Again, the people gathered began to whisper among themselves, and Danny heard Liam Flynn shout, "She's lying!"

"Did you see him?" Danny asked. "Did you see Padraic O'Malley?"

"I went to the seminary with the baby to try to see him. I was out of my mind. He denied us—three times he denied knowing anything about us. He said I was some deranged woman, and the guards came and took us away."

"Then, three years ago, Padraic O'Malley came back into your life," Kelley interrupted her. Danny could see that the garda was finally catching on. "As Father O'Malley, your parish priest and confessor."

Kathleen glanced around the sacristy as if seeking forgiveness from all those gathered. "Desmond and I were so happy before he came here. We loved Ballycara, and I had put the past behind me."

She glanced at Mrs. Slattery. "You know, we had so much trouble getting priests to come here after the previous deaths in the rectory. I was shocked when Padraic was assigned to St. Bridget's. We had not seen each other in twenty-five years. Neither one of us had any idea what had happened to the other. But when he came back, I got all the old bitterness and anger and hatred back. It started to affect my mind." She rubbed her temples as if she had a headache.

"She's crazy," Peggy Malloy murmured.

"Then, to top it off, he kept me from marrying Seamus," she said. "O'Malley ruined my life and then he prevented me from having a family. I wanted to marry Seamus Larkin. We could have been so happy; we both wanted a family; I'm not too old to have another child; we wanted a real family. But O'Malley kept us apart. He knew Michael Conlon was still alive."

"What about Seamus?" Kelley asked. "Did he know about your background?"

Seamus Larkin stepped forward. "I knew nothing about any of this. Why, Kathleen? Why didn't you tell me?"

"And Desmond never knew who his real father was?" Kelley asked.

"Not until yesterday."

"What about you," Kelley said to Nigel. "Did you know Desmond was not your son?"

"I found out when I came here to Ballycara."

"Why *did* you come here?" Kelley asked.

"To see my son and to ask my wife to forgive me for the way I had been. I'm a changed man now."

"So, why have you been passing yourself off as an English tourist?" Danny prompted.

"I didn't want to hurt Kathleen. First, I went to her father in the nursing home. He told me she had been telling everyone all these years that she was a widow and that she wanted to marry this man Seamus Larkin. I didn't come here to spoil her plans. I only wanted to make amends, like the Eighth Step says. I'd made a list of all persons I had harmed and was trying to make amends to them. But I had no idea about Father O'Malley."

Kathleen Conlon stopped him. "Yes, he came to the village and told me he wanted to make amends for the way he had been back then. Said he'd been sober for five years and now he wanted to tell Desmond that he loved him, that he was sorry he was not a good father to him." She turned on Nigel. "Well, I didn't need your apologies, Mick Conlon, or Nigel Greene, or whatever you call yourself now, because you weren't even the father of Desmond."

"Desmond heard us arguing," Nigel added. "He found out the truth."

"And he killed himself," Danny murmured.

"That poor young man," someone in the congregation muttered.

Kelley stepped toward Nigel. "And you killed Father O'Malley from jealousy and anger."

"No," he said. "You don't understand."

"You did!" Kelley said, grabbing Nigel's shoulder.

"For the love of God," Nigel cried out, "tell them, Kathleen."

"I killed him!" Kathleen Conlon shrieked. "I hated him for what he did. And then to spend his life hiding behind a Roman collar. That hypocrite. I hated him!"

Sadness passed over Danny and he hung his head. It hurt to hear the truth about his friend. It seemed he didn't know Father O'Malley as well as he thought he did. That other side of the priest, which he had refused to see, had been exposed to the light of truth.

"He wasn't a hypocrite," Nigel said.

Danny looked up at Nigel.

"He was a good and holy man," Nigel continued, "who had made a mistake in his youth."

"He was a hypocritical bastard," Kathleen hissed.

"It's not true," said Nigel. "After I found out the truth, that I wasn't Desmond's father, I went to see Padraic O'Malley in the rectory. I wanted to help make whatever arrangements could be made. Desmond would have to be taken care of some day. I still felt responsible. That's when Father O'Malley told me that he had been planning to tell Desmond the truth. That he wanted to relieve his guilty conscience. He had been giving Desmond money every month, pretending they were payments for work around the church."

Danny suddenly remembered the cancelled checks written to Desmond he had found among the priest's possessions the day he had searched the rectory.

"Father O'Malley kept talking about the Second Sorrowful Mystery," Nigel continued. "That he'd been saying his rosary all these years, looking for strength to face his past. He wanted forgiveness for what he'd done. Like Christ, who had been scourged and beaten by the Roman soldiers, he said he had to face what was coming to him. He made an appointment to meet with Bishop Hamil. He was going to tell the bishop and the whole parish the truth. At Sunday Mass today he was going to confess to his congregation and ask for forgiveness. He wanted to do the right thing."

So that was what he was planning to tell me, Danny thought, *when we went fishing*. He shook his head. They never did get to catch the biggest brown trout in the River Shannon.

Kathleen's crimson face was streaked with tears. "He was going to shame me and Desmond in front of the whole parish," she screamed. "You think I wanted my son to know he was the child of a Catholic priest? It was too late for that. It would have only hurt Desmond. Oh, yes, Padraic O'Malley waited a little too long to ask for forgiveness." She grinned maliciously. "I killed him, and shut him up forever."

The congregation, gathered at the door of the sacristy, let out a collective growl and pressed forward as if to surround and smother Father O'Malley's murderer.

"Get back," Kelley ordered. "I'll handle this."

"She's insane."

"May she burn in hell!"

"She's a murderer."

Fidelma moved across the sacristy and stood beside Danny while Kathleen wept quietly. Little Jeremy Malloy, still in his altar clothes, looked from one face to another.

"How did you kill him?" Kelley asked.

Kathleen buried her face in her hands.

"May the Lord have mercy on her," said Father Murphy.

Kathleen looked around the sacristy at the faces of the congregation twisted into expressions of anger and outrage.

"How did you do it?" Kelley demanded.

"I took the sedative from your medicine bottle," she said to Nigel. "I noticed you were taking Pamergan for your back pain from the accident years ago. The first time you came to my house you left a bottle on the table and I took it."

She shuddered and held a tissue to her nose. "I was sitting right next to the table of water and wine that morning at Mass. It was easy to drop the Pamergan into the wine during Mass. I was practically touching the table where I sat. I just reached over and dropped it in. Nobody noticed. I could see it working on him throughout the service. After that it was simple. O'Malley was so weak when I got to the sacristy, he could hardly stand. He was just staring at himself in front of his mirror. I took the key from the loop on his belt and led him down into the basement."

Peggy Malloy flew out of the crowd, fingernails raised, and pounced at Kathleen's face. "You sick bitch!" she screamed as Danny and Fidelma grabbed her and held her. Peggy buried her face in Fidelma's shoulder and sobbed.

"What about the herbicide?" Kelley asked, scribbling.

"I had Desmond borrow some from Mrs. Slattery.

He used it in her garden and I got the idea." Kathleen Conlon seemed on the brink of collapse. "Desmond never suspected what I wanted it for."

"And the syringe?"

"Mrs. Larkin, Seamus' mother. She's diabetic, you know. I found the syringes she uses to give herself insulin. I took one."

"How could you do this, Kathleen?" Larkin asked, dumbfounded. He shook his head as if to clear it. "How could you?"

"Let's go," said Kelley, leading Kathleen Conlon from the sacristy.

The mob grudgingly made way, but they glared at Kathleen and hissed insults as Garda Kelley led her away.

"Just one more thing," Kathleen said before she was led from the sacristy. "My boy, Desmond. He knew nothing about any of this."

"But what about the cat?" Danny asked. "He knew about the cat."

"I told him to scare Jeremy. I told him to threaten the boy's cat. He didn't know what he was saying. I told him to scare you, too, with the tractor. He just did what he was told. But I hung the the boy's cat. Desmond had nothing to do with that or the priest's death."

"Come on with you," said Kelley as he moved Kathleen Conlon toward the sacristy door.

Twenty-Three

Danny and Fidelma sat in front of the turf fire that afternoon at Larkin's Pub where most of the village had gathered. Danny propped his head up on his left hand and stared at the fire, his pint of Harp untouched in front of him.

"What's the matter, Danny?" Fidelma asked. "You should be glad you trapped Father's killer."

Danny continued gazing at the fire. He watched the surging flames devour the bricks of turf in the fireplace. "I'm just thinking about Father O'Malley," he said. "I guess he wasn't the man I thought he was."

"Danny," Fidelma said soothingly, "we all make mistakes in our lives."

"But he was a priest!"

"Listen to you," said Fidelma. "A priest is only a man. And Father O'Malley was a good man."

"I want to believe that," Danny said, picking up his pint, "but I don't know if I can now."

"'Judge not,'" she quoted, "'lest you also be judged.'"

"But he deserves some of the blame for what happened."

"Danny, I'm sure he blamed himself every day of his life. That's why he was so obsessed with the Second Sorrowful Mystery of the Rosary. He was lacerating himself with guilt and he died trying to undo the damage he'd done."

"Maybe you're right." Danny's voice quavered. "No one deserves to die the way he did."

"Now we have to forgive him. That's what destroyed Kathleen Conlon's life. She couldn't forgive the people who had wronged her."

"Well, I'll *never* forgive *her*."

"You must, Danny," said Fidelma. "You must pray for her."

"Let me ask you something. Suppose there is a heaven and hell ..."

"Well, of course there is," Fidelma cut in.

"Okay. If there is, do you think ..." Danny turned his pint of Harp in his hand, and looked back into the flickering fire. A brick of turf hissed in the grate as a blue flame snapped and licked at its sides. "I mean, do you think Father O'Malley is going to go to ..."

Fidelma reached out and touched Danny's arm. "Don't, Danny. It's in God's hands now."

"I guess so."

"You know," said Fidelma, "we've been so worried about Father O'Malley, we've nearly forgotten the saddest part of this whole business."

"What's that?"

"Poor Desmond Conlon. You really don't think he knew what his mother was up to?" she asked.

"I don't think he took part in it," Danny said,

shaking his head sadly. "I'm sure he didn't. The way I see it, after Father O'Malley was murdered, Desmond began to suspect what his mother was up to. Then when he heard her arguing with Nigel, and he found out he was Father O'Malley's son, I think he felt somehow responsible for what had happened to the priest and he couldn't live with it, so he committed suicide."

"Maybe he chose Diarmuid and Grainne's Rock," Fidelma continued, "because, like the legend, he was trying to run away from a witch—his mother."

Father Murphy, who sat across the way nursing a whiskey, said, "May the Lord have mercy on her soul." He picked up his drink and carried it over to where Danny and Fidelma sat. "Fidelma, I was wondering if you'd consider coming back and working in the rectory."

Fidelma nibbled her bottom lip. "I don't think so," she said quietly.

"Well, no harm in asking."

Danny squeezed Fidelma's hand. "Now, let me ask you something, Father," he said to the new priest.

"What is it?"

Danny wasn't quite sure how to put it. He looked at Fidelma a moment and said to Father Murphy, "Aren't you a little bit ... paranoid?"

"Paranoid?" the priest asked.

"I mean staying in the rectory. It almost seems like maybe there *is* a curse on the place."

"Well, I've thought of that."

"After all, Father O'Malley is the fourth priest to have died in the rectory."

"Maybe you should consider finding another house," Fidelma said.

"I don't think so," said Father Murphy. "What sort of priest would I appear to be if I let the fairies scare me like that?"

"Then you do believe in them?" Danny asked.

"I didn't say I believed in them," the priest answered. He picked up his whiskey and smiled. "But that doesn't mean they don't exist."

Nearly everyone in the village came up to say goodbye to Danny. Mrs. Slattery planted a kiss on his forehead and said, "Safe home, Danny. And hurry back."

Even Garda Kelley came over. "Thanks for your help," he said.

"Help?" Fidelma repeated. "Danny was the one who—"

Danny reached under the table, touched her hand and she fell silent. "I suppose Kathleen never imagined she would see Padraic O'Malley again after all these years," he said.

"That's what she thought," Kelley answered. "When Father O'Malley was transferred to this parish, sure, it must have been a shock to the both of them. I'm thinking that's what set her off. And then when the husband she had been pretending was dead all these years showed up, she really went 'round the bend. I always knew she wasn't the full shilling."

Fidelma put down her jar of Harp. "I wonder what made the Greenes come back?"

"I've just finished taking statements from them,"

Kelley began. "Apparently Nigel finally realized how sick Kathleen really was and figured out that she did kill Father O'Malley. At first he wanted to leave it all behind, but Eleanor—who isn't, of course, his wife—convinced him to see it through to the end."

"Is he charged with anything?" Danny wanted to know.

Kelley's chest swelled. "Not a bit of it." He cleared his throat. "There's something else I haven't told anyone yet. We searched Desmond's room after we arrested his mother. Found a suicide note."

"He *did* kill himself," Fidelma whispered.

"Looks like it," said Kelley.

"My God," Fidelma added, "she destroyed so many lives."

Kelley said, "I'm afraid Father O'Malley will have to answer to his maker for some of it."

"He was a good man," Danny said. "And a good friend."

"He was," said Fidelma.

"The thing that put me off on the wrong track with James Roche was that Jeremy told me that Roche went into the sacristy to see the priest," Danny said to Fidelma. "I thought for sure he dropped the sedative into the wine then. I was wrong. I wonder why Roche went to see the priest?"

Kelley flashed a superior smile and held his pint of Guinness against his chest. "You have to learn how to question suspects," he began pompously. "You need to draw the information from them, not barrel in there firing questions. A garda is like a priest, you know. People will confess. But you have to let them."

"But Danny was the one—" Fidelma began again before Danny stopped her with a squeeze of the hand.

"Anyway," Kelley continued, "Mr. Roche was very isolated in this village. It's hard living under an assumed identity. He needed to confide in someone, and he figured the priest was the safest person to tell. He wanted to tell the priest who he was and why he was in Ballycara."

"Roche told you that?"

"I learned this from Chief Superintendent Burke," said Kelley as he lifted his pint in farewell and drifted off.

"I can't stand him," Fidelma hissed when Kelley was gone.

"Oh, he's harmless," said Danny, smiling. He glanced at his watch. "Well, I've a bus to catch this afternoon."

"I know," Fidelma whispered.

"When are you going back to Dublin?" he asked.

"I'm ready whenever you are."

Danny looked at her in surprise. "You mean ..."

Fidelma squeezed his hand under the table.

"I've a job interview tomorrow," she said. "There's a secretarial position in the chancery I've been recommended for."

"Good for you, Fidelma. I hope you get it."

Fidelma smiled.

"Shall we ride back together, then?" he asked hopefully.

"Yes."

Father Murphy returned to the table where Danny and Fidelma sat. "You're leaving this afternoon, Danny?"

"That's right."

The priest held the keys to the Nissan Micra out to Fidelma. "Perhaps you'd like to run him up to Dublin."

Fidelma looked at the keys and back to Danny. "We're going back together on the bus," she said.

"I see," said the priest, pocketing the keys.

Fidelma leaned against Danny and said, "Thanks for all you've done for us."

"It was the least I could do for Father O'Malley," he said, putting his arm around her.

Danny saw Peggy Malloy gently guiding Jeremy in their direction. Jeremy approached the table with his hands behind his back.

"I owe you an apology," Danny said to Peggy, but she shook her head vigorously.

"Jeremy has a present for you," she said.

The boy held out a crayon drawing to Danny. In the drawing an oversized man with "Danny" written across his chest held a gun over his head. Kneeling before him was a stick figure. In the right corner the drawing was signed: *To Danny O'Flaherty, Detective. Love Jeremy.*

Danny took the drawing and shook Jeremy's hand. "Thanks, pal."

Peggy put a hand on her son's shoulder.

"Keep in touch," Danny managed.

When they left, Danny pointed at the kneeling figure in the drawing. "I suppose that's Kathleen Conlon?"

"Yes," said Fidelma. "Which makes me wonder. I mean, what will happen to her now?"

Danny flicked his thumb in the direction of Donal Kelley who stood at the bar lecturing a small gathering of villagers on the details of Kathleen Conlon's arrest.

Danny smiled, pulled Fidelma close to him and kissed her. He buried his face in her fragrant red hair and whispered: "It's in Kelley's hands now."